I0695374

Also By Brandon G. Kroupa

The Seventh Year

The Snowball Effect

Saint Nick

The Game Jynx'd

Murder In The Storm

The Demon Of Sweet Briar

What Happened To The "Muth"?

30 Storeys

Stories Within A Story

Brandon G. Kroupa

Chapbook Press

Schuler Books
2660 28th Street SE
Grand Rapids, MI 49512
(616) 942-7330
www.schulerbooks.com

30 Storeys

ISBN 13: 9781966196303

Library of Congress Control Number: 2025915934

Printed in the United States by Chapbook Press.

"It's a long and bumpy road. Embrace the process."

\- Richard Chizmar

Contents

PROLOGUE

Meeting On The 30th Floor

1

Carlton Wolverton can't sleep.

Why, he ponders.

Perhaps it was expecting his upcoming meeting later this morning, or just the simple nervousness of the outcomes of that meeting?

Carlton determines it's a little of both, and sleep is the least of his worries. The meeting that's scheduled at 9 a.m. this morning can determine the course of his future.

A week ago, Carlton received a phone call he never expected. The call was from Stephen Lewis, the head of Chapbook Publishing. It seems one of their big authors had picked up one of Carlton's books at a recent book signing at Charlin's Book Nook in Frankenmuth, Michigan.

Enthusiastically recommending this author, they forwarded it to upper management, suggesting a promising future contribution to Chapbook Publishing.

Currently, Carlton Wolverton is a successful self-published author with seven titles to his name.

Self-publishing, wonderful, yet demanding.

You're the writer, editor, cover designer, and marketer all in one, and they all require considerable amounts of time and work.

Not to mention you handle all expenses.

A major publisher's signature will eliminate many issues, enabling Carlton to pursue his passion—writing—professionally.

Carlton looks at the clock; he observes it's just minutes shy of 7 a.m. The alarm's imminent; embrace it. He propels himself from the bed, eager to get ready.

After a long hot shower and a good shave, Carlton dresses in his best suit.

First impressions are important, and nobody desires a poor start, particularly with such a significant event as this.

As Carlton finishes getting ready, he rehearses possible inquires they may ask. He also checks, rechecks (then checks again) his briefcase to make sure he has everything, including the manuscripts. After one last check, he departs his apartment and makes the half-hour trip to Chapbook Publishing.

2

Carlton makes sure he is early for this meeting. He remembers his teacher Mr. Vander Hyde's philosophy about being on time.

"Late is late," said Mr. Vander Hyde. "If you're on time, you're still late. Fifteen minutes early makes an on-time arrival."

Good words to live by. Carlton walks into the lobby of Chapbook Publishing and approaches the receptionist at the main desk.

"Good morning, sir. How may I assist you?"

"Good morning," says Carlton with a bit of nervousness in his voice. He composes himself, then addresses the receptionist. "My name is Carlton Wolverton. I have a 9 a.m. appointment to speak with Mr. Lewis."

The receptionist types something into the computer and verifies his request.

"Yes, Mr. Wolverton. Mr. Lewis is expecting you," says the receptionist. She points to her right and tells him, "The elevator is right over there. Take it to the 30th floor. You will exit out into a hallway. His office is at the hallway's end on the right."

"Thank you," says Carlton as he makes his way to the elevator.

3

The ascent to the 30th floor seems like an eternity as Carlton watches the floor numbers on the panel change as he passes by each of them. Upon reaching the 30th floor, the elevator seems to hesitate, shakes a bit, then suggests it's about to plummet before the doors open.

A strange sensation, but Carlton figures it is normal for this elevator as he's had similar experiences in the past.

As he gets off the elevator, Carlton heads down the hall, passing many offices. Yet it's the office at the hallway's end that's unique.

The office door has multiple ornate depictions of famous novels carved into it and an opaque window with etching on the glass that reads…

OFFICE OF STEPHEN T. LEWIS
PUBLISHER
Est. April 1974

Carlton takes a deep breath, then opens the door.

He walks into a small waiting room with comfortable furniture. Cozy space; perfect for a book and a hot beverage.

The wall to his left displays awards and pictures of famous authors that Lewis has either meet or is a client of Chapbook Publishing.

The opposite wall has beautiful windows that allow in lots of natural light.

Between them are bookshelves filled with the books that Lewis has helped published throughout the years.

It is a sight to behold. Perhaps Carlton's will be among these in the future, but he is getting ahead of himself. He walks up to Mr. Lewis's secretary and introduces himself.

"Mr. Lewis will be with you in a minute, Mr. Wolverton. May I get you something to drink while you wait?"

"No thank you, I'm fine."

Carlton takes a seat until Mr. Lewis emerges from his office.

"Mr. Wolverton, I presume," says Mr. Lewis.

"You presume correctly, Mr. Lewis," replies Carlton, "And please, call me Carlton," extending his hand to Mr. Lewis.

Mr. Lewis shakes Carlton's hand and tells him, "It is a pleasure to meet you, Carlton, and you may call me Stephen. We try to keep it as informal as possible as it is more relaxing and less stressful. Come on in and let's chat," motioning Carlton into his office.

Carlton breathes a sigh of relief. It's time for his self-promotion and book pitch.

4

Three Hours Later.

The door to Stephen Lewis's office opens as he escorts Carlton out.

He shakes Carlton's hand and tells him, "Carlton, thank you for coming in this morning and enlightening me about your work and your background. I believe you'll thrive at Chapbook Publishing, and I'm eager to work alongside you. Expect contact from an agent to discuss specifics."

"Thank you, Stephen. It has been a pleasure, and I look forward to working with you and Chapbook Publishing. Have a good day."

Carlton thanks Stephen's secretary as well and bids her a good day before departing the office.

5

Carlton walks to the elevator and pushes the button to call it. He cannot believe his luck. His dream is on the verge of coming true.

The elevator doors open to reveal that it is empty. Entering, he presses "L" for the lobby. He clenches his fist, raises it in the air and brings it down, blurting out an emphatic "YES" as the doors close.

Carlton doesn't notice that the elevator isn't moving because he's too preoccupied with his upcoming publication.

On top of that, he received a three-book deal. These books, unlike the self-published ones, will have deadlines over the next couple of years. This new challenge awaits Carlton, a challenge he's ready for.

Carlton notices the elevator isn't going anywhere, so he pushes the button for the lobby again.

A momentary pause precedes the elevator's ascent, which breaks off.

A cracking and snapping sound occur as Carlton feels his stomach drop, the feeling like the first drop of a roller coaster after hitting its peak at the start of the ride.

Carlton realizes the elevator cables have snapped, and the elevator is in free fall. Why the emergency breaks haven't kicked in to stop the fall, he doesn't know. All he is aware of is that he's falling thirty stories to his demise.

This should take seven to ten seconds to happen. However, time seems to have no meaning as the floors pass by. Carlton wonders about the story he can tell if he survives this.

Wait, story? He thinks to himself. No. Stories!

As the light for the 30th floor extinguishes, the light for the 29th floor illuminates Carlton's mind occupies itself with coming up with a story for this floor and every floor thereafter instead of thinking about his last moments…

29TH
FLOOR

Move... Or Get Run Over!

Peter is one hellion of an eight-year-old. He doesn't look like it, nor does he act like it. You won't know until you get acquainted with him.

One of his favorite things to do is to jump on his BMX dirt bike and tear down his Petoskey home's two-track driveway. He banks it hard out onto Jefferson Road, praying he doesn't wipe out or have an oncoming car hit him (rare as the street is quiet). He watches the sparks fly from the pedal as it contacts the street.

From there Peter rides down Jefferson, makes a quick right turn onto Pearl, and then hits Washington at high speed, riding down to a little party store known as Tom & Dick's.

Once there, he spends his allowance on comics, movie collector cards, and, of course, every kid's delicacy... candy.

Peter's parents warn him all the time that if he doesn't pay better attention, he can hurt himself or someone else from the neighborhood. He cares not either way. Peter knows what he's doing. No way anything can happen.

Why you ask?

Because prior to taking off, Peter always walks to the end of the driveway. He makes sure everything is clear before he even attempts it. Otherwise, even if the coast is clear, his sister Beatrice, who plays out in the front yard, will warn him.

This may seem like any normal day. *Not* a normal day, mind you. Expect someone to say, *"I told you so."*

Peter goes out front to check things out. As usual, nothing is going on.

"Beatrice, I'm going for a ride. Let me know if anything's coming," Peter says, going to get his bike.

As he heads for the sidewalk near the back porch, Beatrice stops what she is doing and walks towards the driveway. She sees Peter walk the bike over to the driveway from where he had parked it.

Peter moves into position and gets on. He yells, "AM I CLEAR?" to his sister.

"CLEAR!" she yells back.

A second later, Peter gives the pedal a good shove with his foot and he's off. He picks up the speed he wants in quick fashion.

What happens next is nothing more than an act of sheer stupidity. Beatrice jumps into his path.

"I'M NOT MOVING!" she tells him.

"I'M NOT STOPPING!" responds Peter.

The warning and ultimatum come within seconds of Peter plowing over his sister. He told her he wasn't stopping. She warned him she wasn't moving.

The collision with his sister sends him flying up and over the bike's handlebars. Peter lands hard on his back, sliding a few feet before coming to a stop.

Beatrice gets the worst of it.

When the bike contacts her, it throws her to the side, the spinning tire burning a track mark across her forehead. She screams in pain.

Hearing the screams from inside the house, Peter's father bursts out the front door.

"What's going on out here?!" he yells, rushing to Beatrice.

"Peter ran me over," screams Beatrice as the fake tears roll down her cheek. "I told him to stop, but he wouldn't."

He makes sure Beatrice is fine, then goes over to Peter. Peter grimaces in pain as his father hauls him up off the ground. He knows he'll feel this later. His father scolds him. "You're in serious trouble, young man! How many times do we have to tell you to stop and pay attention? You're grounded, Peter!"

"Dad," says Peter. "Will you let me explain…"

"I don't want to hear it," says his father, not willing to listen as he drags Peter towards the door.

"Well then, you'll hear it from me," says a voice from behind him.

His father turns around to see his mother standing on the front porch. Her expression reveals trouble for his father.

"Beatrice is as much at fault as he is," she tells him.

"I doubt that. You realize he did this on purpose," says Peter's father.

"No, he didn't," replies Peter's mother. "I watched the whole thing unfold. Your darling daughter, whom you see as faultless, jumped right in front of him. She's aware he tears out of here all the time on his bike."

"That doesn't excuse him for not trying to stop."

"I agree, however, Beatrice played the game of '*chicken*' and Peter called her on it."

"Is this true, Beatrice?" asks her father.

Beatrice doesn't answer.

"Is it?" he asks again, more forcefully.

"Yes," says Beatrice in a whimper.

He goes over and picks Peter's bike up from the ground. "You're both grounded. Go inside and clean yourselves up now!"

Peter watches his dad chuck his bike into the backyard as he walks up the steps to the porch. He tells his mother as he passes her on his way into the house, "Told her I wasn't stopping."

28TH
FLOOR

Michigan Theory

Michigan. The thirty-eighth state of our union. The Great Lakes State. A state known around our great country for things such as the auto industry, furniture, Motown, and the birthplace of many talented actors and memorable musicians.

Weather in Michigan is a mess. Not uncommon in Michigan for us to have all four seasons in mere hours. How Michiganders (what we call ourselves) deal with it is the difference between night and day.

I've lived in Michigan my entire life. How *do* Michiganders deal with the weather, especially rain and snow? I have my personal theory. Would you like to hear it?

Okay, pull out a map of Michigan. Forget the upper peninsula. That's its own animal. Focus on the lower peninsula. Now, divide the lower peninsula in half. Your line should run through the city of Big Rapids, if not use US 10.

Now my theory has two parts. One for rain, the other for snow.

Let's start with the rain first.

North of Big Rapids, or above the line you drew, when it rains everyone goes out. They go shopping; out to eat; see a movie; or to do whatever it is they do when it rains. Why go out in the rain? The answer, up North: during the rain, means no walking the beach or hiking wooded trails; sailing the lake; golfing; or whatever activity you enjoy doing during the beautiful weather.

Make sense so far?

It would be logical to assume (which you should never do) south of Big Rapids, or below the line you drew, this would also hold true. Guess what, my friends, it doesn't. South of Big Rapids, when it rains, people don't go out. They stay in. Unlike up north, malls, restaurants, even movie theatres are dead. No one is around. Everyone south of that line fears the rain like the Wicked Witch of the West.

I bet you're scratching your head right now thinking about it, especially if you live in Michigan. You know what I speak of is true. My theory of snow you will find also to be true.

Snow holds the opposite effect in both areas.

In Michigan, when a snow event in the northern part of the lower peninsula occurs, it comes down with a vengeance. Not uncommon for four to six inches of snow to fall during each system that comes through. Can be worse. Got to love lake effect! People are used to getting lots of snow. Therefore, they get what they need, then hunker down until the snow stops. After the snow stops falling, they dig out, then go out.

Not to say that when it snows south of Big Rapids that the southern part of the lower peninsula doesn't get its fair share of snow, just affects people in the opposite manner.

Snow south of Big Rapids translates to go out and see how much carnage you can cause. People are itching to get out! They go to the mall; out to eat; to the movies; make a return to a store. The list is endless. They endanger themselves, their kids, and others, depending on how bad it is. Simple madness is what I call it! No logic at all!

It's crazy how the two halves of the lower peninsula deal with rain and snow. I won't even hypothesize a theory for the upper peninsula. Again, I have lived in Michigan my entire life, living in both the northern and southern parts of the lower peninsula. If you *also* dwell in the state, you know my theory holds true.

Think about it. I bet you will come to the same conclusion.

Otherwise… prove me wrong.

27TH
FLOOR

The Turkey Tradition

1

Funny story, at least I think it is. As I pass the 27th floor, it reminds me of a particular Thanksgiving that fell on the 27th of November, back when I was a junior in high school. Quite a coincidence, don't you think?

I digress. In my English class, our teacher assigned us a writing assignment where we were to write an original story about the traditions of Thanksgiving. It was also to be an oral presentation to the class.

Oh, she shouldn't have done that one. She let loose a comedian with this one, so here goes…

2

Everyone knows the story of Thanksgiving. Pilgrims made their way to the new world, landing on Plymouth Rock in 1620. The next year, they celebrated the first "Thanksgiving" feast with the Indians after the harvest. You are familiar with the tale.

Are you also aware that they enjoyed turkey at this feast? This is indeed the case.

Turkeys, however, were not native to America. They were native to Europe in a country we know today as… Turkey. Yes, my friends, the turkey came from Turkey!

Like the Pilgrims, the birds fled their native land for the New World, hoping to live free without the fear of being hunted and eaten. It's a matter of historical record that these sly birds hitched a ride on the

Mayflower in secret, led by the fastest, biggest, and brightest of them all. An elegant tom, named A. Gobbler.

After arriving in the New World, A. Gobbler led his flock deep into the woods far from the Pilgrims establishment. He counted on the Pilgrims not straying too far from their homes. What A. Gobbler didn't account for were the indigenous Indians that also lived in the same woods he had brought his flock to.

Pheasants were a good meal; however, the Indians saw the turkey as a dumb bird, thus making it an easier meal to catch. They would soon learn the opposite was true.

The Indians found it was no simple task to catch these birds. Because of the difficulty in catching them, the Indians hunted them once a year, in autumn. Think of it as an ancient form of deer season.

As the first Thanksgiving was being planned, the Indian chief told the Pilgrims of the turkey, and insisted they include this tasteful bird in their feast.

Since the Pilgrims didn't have the knowledge on how to catch the turkey, the chief called upon his most skilled warrior. One with great patience and the most successful at catching these birds. He was the elite warrior… Me-A-Catchum!

Me-A-Catchum had splendid success hunting the turkey. His task, catch a turkey like no other for this feast. A turkey which had eluded him and others from the tribe. The great turkey, A. Gobbler.

3

At dawn, Me-A-Catchum set out to find A. Gobbler.

He tracked him for days until one afternoon he found A. Gobbler near a river in a great valley. When the chance presented itself, Me-A-Catchum moved in for the kill.

It was no effortless task.

For hours, Me-A- Catchum pursued A. Gobbler, shooting arrows, chucking tomahawks, and anything else he could use as a weapon, to no avail. All of them missed by mere inches because of A. Gobbler's cunning and swift moves.

As dusk approached, a vision came to him from noble warriors who had passed into spirit. They spoke to him, telling him of a secret weapon that would allow him to catch the elusive bird.

Me-A-Catchum took two medium-sized stones and tied each one to opposite ends of a short rope. He then tied a longer rope in the center of the shorter one between the two stones. The weapon ready, he resumed the hunt.

It wasn't long before he came upon the magnificent bird.

Me-A-Catchum moved in stealthily. At the right moment, he cried out. "A. GOBBLER! ME-A-CATCHUM!"

The magnificent bird was quick and elusive. It didn't suspect the new weapon.

At that precise moment, Me-A-Catchum twirled the weapon above his head, throwing it at A. Gobbler. He threw the weapon quick. He threw it low.

It twirled, making a whistling sound as it flew, finding its target… the legs of the magnificent bird.

Upon impact, it wrapped around A. Gobbler's legs, tripping him up. He fell to the ground with a thud. Seconds later, Me-A-Catchum caught up to him, tomahawk in hand, ready for the kill.

4

Me-A-Catchum returned to his village with the magnificent bird. Presenting the bird to the chief, he stated, "Me caught-um."

"So you did," replied the chief.

The tribe cooked the magnificent bird and took it to the feast where it would become a tradition every Thanksgiving hence forth.

However, eating the magnificent bird came with a curse. The Indians called it sleeping sickness because after consuming turkey; you get sleepy.

We know it as tryptophan… A. Gobbler's curse to the world for finally being caught.

26TH
FLOOR

Shooter's Trivia Tuesday

1

Shooter's Bar is one of those little hole-in-the-wall establishments in one of the rougher neighborhoods in downtown Chicago.

The owners of the establishment will tell you… Don't judge a book by its cover.

While unassuming on the outside, the inside is quite different.

Inside is the city's best bar. Burgers to die for. Décor from a bygone era. And a trivia night that rivals all. Tuesday's ideal. That's what many say.

"Really," says Steve. "Is that why you've dragged me into this low-life neighborhood tonight?"

"You said you wanted a good burger and wanted to play trivia," explains Mark. "This place does both. It combines top-tier burgers with exceptional trivia for a perfect night. Not to mention you could win some serious coin."

"Mark, I'm going to give you the benefit of the doubt tonight. You'll be in trouble if this place doesn't live up to its reputation, my friend."

Mark isn't pleased with Steve's attitude towards the situation. Though he knows he'll be the one having the last laugh.

2

Mark and Steve make their way inside Shooter's Bar and are in awe of what they see. As advertised, the outside looks like a rat hole. However, the inside is a sight to be admired.

You're transported back in time to a nostalgic, pristine 1940s era club complete with all the trimmings. The patron's dress contrasts with the staff who wear period costumes. Management even appears as mob bosses from the era.

Steve tells Mark as they take their seats, "You were right about this place. This is spectacular."

A server approaches them and asks with a thick Chicago accent, "What'll you have, gentlemen?"

Without looking at a menu, Steve responds, "I'll take one of your famous burgers and a house beer."

"How do you like your burger cooked?" she asks.

"Rare, sweetheart," says Steve, smitten with her.

"And for you, love?" she asks Mark.

"I'll take the same, thank you," he answers.

"Anything else I can get you, gentlemen?"

"Yes. How do we get into the trivia bout tonight?" asks Steve.

"I'll let the boss know you are interested," she tells him as she walks away with a cute little strut that doesn't go unnoticed by Steve.

Steve watches as she approaches the bartender and says something to him. The bartender then motions to someone else. That someone comes over, leans in, then heads over to their table.

"Good evening, gentlemen. My name is Vincent Grubauer. I am the owner of this establishment. It is my understanding you wish to partake in our trivia contest this evening?"

"Yes, we would, sir," says Mark.

"I like you," says Vincent. "A gentleman knows his manners! Alright then. It's a twenty-dollar cover charge to play. Fifty dollars, if you would like what we call the extras. The rules are simple. Answer correctly, you move on to the next round. Fail, you lose and are out."

"And what are those extras, Mr. Grubauer?" asks Steve.

"The extras, gentlemen, are twofold. Risk and reward. Think of it as Russian roulette. Wager on who you think will get shot, so to speak, during the tournament. You might get shot. Be a real bad ending to your evening. That's the risk."

"And the reward?" asks Mark.

"My good man, a triple jackpot awaits you if you correctly pick the person who makes the final round and gets shot."

"Sounds interesting," says Steve. "Let's go for it. The whole thing."

"Are you absolutely sure, my friend?" says Vincent.

"With no doubt, sir," says Steve.

"Your funeral, my friend," Vincent tells him as he motions for one of his fellow workers.

An associate brings a pen tucked inside a small booklet. He opens it up and presents it to both Steve and Mark.

"This is our standard contract for the game," Vincent informs them. "There is also a waiver to sign that absolves us from all transgressions. Please read them both carefully, as they are legal and binding."

Steve is all in and signs without reading either of them.

Mark, unlike most others, reviews the documents before signing, following Mr. Grubauer's advice.

After their signatures are complete, Vincent gives them a nod of approval as the server brings their meals.

"Enjoy your burgers, gentlemen," he tells them. "They could be the last meal you eat. Trivia starts at 9 p.m. sharp," and walks away.

"What did he mean by that?" asks Steve.

"Part of the drama and play of this place," responds Mark as he covers his burger in a thick coat of ketchup.

3

9 p.m. rolls around and the showmanship of the establishment takes over.

LADIES AND GENTLEMEN!
WELCOME TO SHOOTER'S TRIVIA TUESDAY!

The crowd cheers at the announcement.

Vincent Grubauer takes the mic to tell those assembled, "Tonight we have ten brave souls ready to compete on our grand trivia stage. Each contestant received an electronic pad to answer each question. Everyone knows the rules. Answer correctly, you move on. Answer incorrectly, you're out! Now, five of our participants have elected to go for the extras… who gets shot during the game!"

The crowd goes wild at this announcement. The extras always get selected on Tuesday evenings.

"We have provided a separate pad for each of you brave souls. We have assigned each of you a random number. Please choose a number between one and nine of whom you believe will be the one to be shot. You may do so now."

Vincent signals all participants have locked in their responses. Next, he declares, "Audience members not playing bet on a contestant's demise, and win cash! We will take wagers for the next five minutes."

4

Five Minutes Later.

"All wagers are now closed," announces Vincent. "Charlie, please take it from here."

"Yes, sir," says Charlie. "Let the game… BEGIN! Please draw your attention to the big screen."

The big screen's curtains open displaying the words

ROUND 1

"Here is your first question," announces Charlie as it comes up.

```
Harrison Ford was not George Lucas and
Steven Spielberg's first choice for the
     role of Indiana Jones. Who was...


A. Burt Reynolds
B. Tom Selleck
C. John Wayne
D. Richard Chamberlain
```

A timer counts down as the ten participants lock in their answer.

"Time," announces Charlie. "The correct answer is B. Tom Selleck. Because of his role as Thomas Magnum on the hit show Magnum, P.I., he had to decline the part. Nine of ten answered the question correctly."

"Do we have someone being shot in this round?" asks Charlie.

After a very tense moment, nothing happens.

"It appears this is not the round," announces Charlie.

A chorus of boos echoes from the crowd. Everyone here this evening was hoping for an immediate shooting.

"Don't worry, my friends," says Charlie. "Just means extra value for you all! Next round!"

Shooter's Trivia Contest continues over the next hour.

The remaining players whittle down while the crowd grows restless without a Shooter's Victim.

5

The contest comes down to just Steve and Mark. The tension between them... at an all-time high.

"We are down to two participants," says Charlie. "Two friends, no less. Isn't this poetic justice? Someone will shoot one of these two lads! It's time for SUDDEN DEATH!"

The crowd cheers with excitement. They expect this every Tuesday night.

"Here is your last question of the night, gentlemen," Charlie informs them.

The trailer for the 1998 film Les
Misérables highlights the main cast as
Academy Award winners or nominees, except
for which actor/actress?

```
A. Liam Neeson
B. Geoffrey Rush
C. Uma Thurman
D. Claire Danes
```

Steve knows this one right after reading it and locks in his answer in seconds. Mark, though, takes a minute pondering the question before he locks in his answer.

An uncomfortable silence falls over the bar as Charlie hesitates.

He informs the crowd, "We have a winner! The correct answer is D. Claire Danes. After the others received their accolades, they introduced Claire Danes as Cosette. Which means you, sir, are tonight Shooter's Trivia Tuesday winner!" says Charlie, raising Steve's hand in victory.

As Steve gloats, a man dressed to resemble a 1940s hitman comes out. He saunters up to Mark and pulls a gun, pointing it at his head.

Steve is in shock as he realizes right then, this is the real deal. It's not fake. He is about to watch his friend die when the unexpected happens.

The hitman moves the gun from Mark's temple, aims right at Steve's head, and pulls the trigger. The bullet rips through his skull. Steve drops to the floor with a thud.

The crowd roars with applause as Mark stands there and laughs.

Vincent comes over to congratulate Mark. "Well played, my friend! Let me buy you a drink."

As he escorts Mark to the bar, he tells Charlie, "Get someone over here to take care of this mess."

Charlie nods in acknowledgment. He snaps his fingers for two men to come over and remove Steve's dead body.

Mark may have lost the match, but he won the jackpot. More importantly, he's the one having the last laugh, just as he knew he would.

25TH
FLOOR

Gordie Dyer

1

Sleep doesn't come easy tonight for Gordie Dyer. There are few nights that it does. Since having that strange dream a couple of weeks before, sleep seems like a memory. A memory long forgotten.

He looks at the clock. "Time," he speaks in a dry tone. The apartment's central computer projects 6:25 a.m. into a suspended mist above the bed. Gordie sighs, knowing full well the alarm to start the routine of the day will harp out in *exactly* five minutes. What to do? Lie there and wait for the inevitable? Break routine and get going?

Gordie goes for the latter.

Throwing back the covers, his movement triggers the automated lights built into the room. They glow dim because of the time. Gordie swings his legs over the edge of the bed and stretches. Getting out of bed, he trudges slowly towards the only window in the room. It is medium, rectangular and stretches close to the full length of the wall. At first glance, it looks like the wall until Gordie utters the word "Shades," again in that dry voice of his. In similar fashion to the lights, the shades built inside the window open at a snail's pace, allowing in the grey, gloomy light of the morning.

Gordie stands there and looks out at the Blackhaven skyline. All that his eye, or anyone's eye can see, is nothing more than endless buildings, upon buildings, all similar in structure… straight edged, sharp corners, all bleak in appearance.

What lies outside the city? Gordie has no clue and wonders if *anyone* does? The logical and correct answer is *no*. The leaders of the city, The Axis, make it clear Blackhaven is "infinite". If anyone knows or sees what's outside the city, they'll never admit it. It isn't a good idea to go against The Axis's wisdom. Only those from an older generation know what lies outside the city. They are long since gone.

Time to stop focusing on unimportant things as Gordie realizes he is off schedule.

2

Getting ready in the morning isn't much of an issue. With all the technology Gordie has at his disposal, it takes less than ten minutes to shit, shower, and shave. He dresses and is in the kitchen, having his morning cup of coffee and toast in no time.

Tapping the counter brings up a small screen. On it, Gordie listens to the news (provided by The Axis) while he reviews the day's events. They include update the boss, plan the day with his team, then write the instructions and lay out the specs on the latest technological innovation. His latest project is one he looks forward to owning: an automated chef.

The idea is rather simplistic: toss all your ingredients in, no measurements required, and it will produce the perfect meal every time in a matter of minutes. Gordie is optimistic that he and his team can get that down to seconds. However, between timing problems and issues with the food's appearance, there are just certain laws of physics you can't alter. Tastes great, looks like absolute shit. *But hey, beggars can't be choosers, they say.*

Gordie is far from a beggar. He's done well for himself. He is intellectually gifted, has a pleasant apartment, makes good money, and has a good number of those technological luxuries. Though Gordie isn't rich, he doesn't have to scrape to get by.

He wonders, *Is there more to life? Perhaps someone to share this with?* He immediately dismisses the thought. Being to set in his routine, remaining single is the logical option.

The dream he had a couple of weeks back attempts to creep back into his thoughts. A chime signaling *time to leave* cuts it short. The dream will have to wait. Right now, Gordie needs to get going. He picks up his briefcase and grabs his jacket as he makes his way down the stairs, out the door, and onto the street to catch the transport to work.

3

The transports in Blackhaven are spot on accurate with their time of arrival. They're never late… ever! You can set your watch by them and never be off. Breakdowns also never occur because of a very scrutinized daily diagnostic.

They also enforce strict guidelines to pinpoint the precise moment you need to arrive at make your specific destination on time. Arrive late… you wait for the next transport, which then makes you late to your destination. Being late is not acceptable, nor an option, especially if it is for work. If you are late for work, consider yourself screwed.

Society has conformed to not being late. Those who are… it doesn't bode well for them. Gordie is always on time. He's always early and never misses the transport. Those that know him suspect he may be an actual robot, an actual piece of technology of Blackhaven. It is absurd, but it still makes him the ideal citizen.

The transport arrives exactly as scheduled.

Gordie boards at the precise time and within minutes, he's making his way into Colony, one of the prime technology producers in the city.

Gordie goes over to one of the check-in terminals located inside the entrance. He leans over the device, placing his right eye to an infrared scanner.

The scanner activates and reads his unique retinal print.

Once the scanner verifies Gordie's identity, the terminal prints out a detailed schedule of Gordie's itinerary for the day as set forth by Colony's upper management.

It reads…

ITINERARY: GODIE DYER
Tuesday, July 17, 2525

8:00am – 8:10am:
Prep For The Day

8:15am – 8:30am:
Meeting (Boss)

8:35am – 8:40am:
Meeting (Team)

8:45am – 12:00pm:
Tech Writing

12:00pm – 12:15pm:
Lunch

12:15pm – 12:30pm:
Personal Time

12:30pm – 3:00pm:
Tech Sketches

3:05pm – 3:55pm:
Day Summary (Boss/Team)

4:00pm – 5:00pm:
Cleanup/Prep Next Day

Everything is precise and always on schedule. No time wasted. Nothing runs over, and if it does, you'll be playing that most wonderful of all games, *Let's Catch Hell Today!* A game you don't want to play because the Colony runs it on a two-strike system. Strike one, you catch Hell. Strike two, you go to Hell. Bye-bye, see you later. You're unemployed! Have a *nice* day.

Gordie, though, is a model employee of Colony. He is that robot, damn close to perfect in every way. Or so he thinks.

4

Gordie walks to his well laid out, efficient office cubicle and performs his morning prep right up to the second before he must leave for his daily meeting with the boss. He grabs a cup of coffee before he enters the office of his boss, Mr. Fitz Dominic. Mr. Dominic is in his early fifties and a beanpole. This is one boss who lives up to his name. Piss him off and he'll throw fits! This is of no concern to Gordie. Fitz considers him one of his best and brightest. Gordie is so logical that if Fitz has some sort of issue, he can set him at ease before he goes off.

Fitz is sitting at his desk when Gordie enters. "Good Morning, Mr. Dyer. What is the plan for the day?" He doesn't even look up from his computer.

"Get with the team on production. Work on the tech writing. Based on that, work on the respective sketches based on the writing. Analysis of what's been done. Prep for tomorrow based on today's accomplishments or issues," says Gordie, all answers short and to the point.

"Good. Anything else to report?" asks Fitz.

"No, Mr. Dominic. Anything for the team?"

"Tell them to have all parts ready for inspection at day's end. Providing they meet the required specifications, and I know they will, we can get the prototype built before week's end," Fitz informs him. Then he adds, "Also, tell them I don't want this to end up like Foley's project."

"Yes, sir. Anything else?"

"No. I'll get your analysis at 3:05 p.m. That is all."

Without another word, Gordie leaves precisely a minute before he needs to. There's nothing quite like being ahead of schedule. It's a great feeling.

5

The team meeting should move at the same pace as his meeting with Fitz.

It doesn't though.

Zachary Hunter, a new employee of Colony, continually asks unnecessary questions about the Foley Project instead of qualified ones about the project at hand.

By the time Gordie and the team have set him straight, and they address all relative questions, it is 8:40 a.m.

Throw being ahead of the schedule out the window.

6

Gordie moves with urgency back to his office cubicle. He makes it back with a little over two minutes of leeway. Back ahead of the game, just the way he likes it. He sits down at his computer, which automatically fires up while he preps his gear: a small headphone-like device that acts like a mind reader. The device instantaneously transmits your thoughts to the computer, wording them in perfect form. No misinterpretations, no ideas withheld. Focus on thinking, allow the device to do the rest, are Colony's wishes. Efficiency at its best.

A select few, like Gordie, are so tech savvy they can write it themselves just as efficiently, but that's not permitted.

Gordie gets into his rhythm almost immediately. He is well on a roll with his technical writing, or so he thinks. After a few minutes, something is different. His thoughts stray from their technical norm. This automated chef he's working on takes on a life of its own. A life not at all technical.

This automated chef isn't so automated after all. It's an actual person. One that is fun, exciting, and vivid in every way, shape, and form. Descriptions of how it prepares the food are in exact detail. The smells, flavors, and textures described in a way that makes his mouth water and wants the concoction described.

Suddenly, Gordie stops. He reads his last sentence in absolute fear. It reads…

Cooking is a lost "art" form.

He reads it again to make sure his eyes aren't deceiving him. They aren't. Even the device he wears interprets his thoughts the same way as typed on the screen. Gordie had been thinking about "Art"!

Oh, shit! This is terrible, Gordie.

Gordie rips the device from his head and throws it aside. In a near state of panic, he jumps out of his seat and begins pacing back and forth in what space there is in his office cubicle.

"Calm down, Gordie," he tells himself. "There's a logical explanation for this. There must be."

Taking a deep breath, Gordie slows his mind to determine what the problem is. Then it hits him. It was that dream he had. That is it. That dream that kept him from sleeping has messed up his mind. Problem found, shake it off, find a solution.

Sitting back down, Gordie places the device back on his head and clears his thoughts. He goes over what he's written to find the exact point where he flew off kilter. The moment he finds it; he immediately deletes everything from that point on. Must get rid of the evidence. But what if his superiors saw? What then? They closely monitor everything at the Colony.

Gordie is brilliant, though. The best course of action… purge the "art" from his thoughts and any remaining in the specs. Perfect, the written work before the glitch, and move forward. If asked, and that probability exists, even if it is unlikely (because of his spotless and perfect record), Gordie can explain it away logically as either a "block" or an inadequate amount of sleep. Both conditions occur to the best tech writers from time to time. So, no harm, no foul.

Gordie realizes he can make up the lost time, once explained. This eases Gordie's mind as he gets back on track.

As lunch draws near, Gordie finishes up this part of his day. A simple yet petrifying thought creeps into his mind as he finishes up. *What if this happens again?* Or the worst-case scenario, *what if this continues to happen?*

Questions Gordie trusts he will never have to answer.

24TH
FLOOR

You're A Poor Excuse For A Pavlovian Dog

Ray leans against the counter, arms crossed, looking bored out of his mind. No one's in the store, not even a peep in the parking lot. And why should there be? It's your typical Sunday morning. Everyone's still sleeping or sitting in church. It'll get busier soon. For now, there's nothing to do but stand around, twiddle your thumbs, and wait for someone to grace the store with their presence.

As he walks around the counter, the doorbell sounds. Lost in boredom, he doesn't acknowledge the person entering. Typically, this isn't an issue, but in this case, it is a major mistake, as it involves Amir, the store's owner.

Amir, a middle-aged man of Middle Eastern descent, struts into the store, dressed in a stylish, yet ill-fitting suit. Although he portrays himself as being an intellectual business owner, Amir is nothing more than a simple farmer who has great people skills. He walks over to Ray, but his face betrays his calm demeanor. He stands there as Ray putters along, still failing to acknowledge anyone is even in his presence.

"Ah-hem," Amir utters, clearing his throat to make his presence known.

Startled by the sound, Ray snaps out of his daze and acknowledges him. "Hello, Amir. I didn't even hear you come in."

"Perhaps I need to turn the volume up on the bell so you can, Ray," says Amir in his thick accent. "There's a reason I put that bell in. Do you know what that reason is by chance?" he asks.

"No, I don't," Ray responds in a sarcastic tone. "But I'm sure that you're about to remind me why."

"I don't like your attitude, Ray," snaps Amir. "It's so you know when a customer enters the store."

"I usually do," Ray tells him. "Guess I was in a daze and wasn't paying attention like I normally would."

"Ray, you must do better! The customer is very important. The bell signifies a customer's presence in our store. As the bell rings," he leans in and whispers to Ray, "Be like a Pavlovian dog." He jumps, turning towards the door and says in a louder voice, "Greet the customer with a resounding WELCOME TO THE VIDEO STATION!"

Ray stands there in utter disbelief, looking at Amir as if he has just lost all his marbles. He asks, "Did you just call me a Pavlovian dog?"

"No, I said you must act like a Pavlovian dog when you hear that bell and welcome the customer! It is very important."

"So, you want me to act like a Pavlovian dog now? What exactly is a Pavlovian dog?"

"Allah, forgive him!" Amir cries as he looks up at the ceiling. "What are they teaching you in these schools these days?! My God!" he blurts out. Regaining his composure, he explains to Ray that "Pavlov was a scientist who trained a dog to salivate upon hearing the ringing of a bell. Get the connection I'm trying to get across?"

Ray stands there speechless for a moment. Then, in a smart, cocky tone says, "So you want me to salivate when the bell rings? As I am excited by the customer's arrival, I turn and yell WELCOME TO THE VIDEO STATION," imitating Amir's previous actions.

"YES!" screams Amir, like a little girl. "You've got it!"

"You're whacked, Amir," says Ray, "You know that, right?" His words dripping with bitterness as he confronts Amir, who stands there smug, basking in the insult rather than being offended.

Ray shakes his head and chuckles. "What do you have in the bag, Amir?" he asks, noticing the bag that Amir carries at his side.

"Ah, yes. Something else I want to bring to your attention," he says, emptying the contents of the bag all over the counter.

From the bag, aside from a horrific odor, slide shreds of paper covered in goo and other foreign substances. Ray backs up in disgust. "You've struck it rich, Amir, and found trash! What a discovery!"

"NO! It's not trash!" he insists. "It's recycle! I found this in the trash!"

"So you went dumpster diving in the trash to find trash? I see."

"I don't think you do, Ray," Amir tells him. "See, you should have recycled this, not thrown it in the trash. Do you realize we have a responsibility to the planet? If it's recyclable, then it needs to be put in the recycle bin! It's that easy. Don't be lazy and toss it in the trash!"

"Okay, Amir," Ray says, agreeing with Amir just to get him off his back. "Amir, it's now disgusting because of being mixed with the trash. Unfortunately, it needs to go back in the trash."

"No!", says Amir, "Bruce, Nikki, and Lindsay need to see this. I'm certain that one of them is behind this because they're all lazy."

"Well, Amir, it'll have to wait. Hate to break it to you, but I have some bad news for you."

"What is it?" he asks.

"They all called off for their shifts today."

"What do you mean, they all called off today? I told them they had to work today because I gave all of them yesterday off for their dance."

"Well, you may have told them they were working today," Ray explains, "but they all called off, anyway. I assume they're all hurting from the dance they attended last night. Partied a bit too much, I think."

Amir stands speechless for a moment. His face turns red and puffy, like a volcano on the brink of eruption. A moment later he yells, "GODDAMN IIIITTTT!!! I give them the entire day off yesterday, and then being the nice guy that I am, I schedule them later today so that they could enjoy their dance and what do they do? I'll tell you what they do. They screw me over! Damn them! Never again! Next time they ask for something like this, tough luck!"

"Well, you have no worries, Amir," Ray tells him in a very reassuring voice. "I'm here today and so is Casey. So, we're good."

"Ah, yes. You two are always dependable. You're both good Muslims," he adds.

"Why am I a good Muslim even though I'm not one?" Ray asks.

"Because Ray. All good Muslims work on Sundays. It's a favorite saying of mine. You and Casey, both here working today, are good Muslims. Those who called off, not so much."

"Not only am I a good Muslim," says Ray with little enthusiasm and sarcasm, "I'm also required to salivate like a Pavlovian dog. Great."

The doorbell chimes. The day's first customer arrives.

Ray, mocking Amir's previous demonstration, turns towards the door, spitting a bit as he does, and exclaims to the customer coming in the door, "WELCOME TO THE VIDEO STATION!" all wide-eyed and spazzed out as he does.

The customer looks at Ray in shock. Amir gleefully yells, "YES! You've got it!" as the customer promptly turns and exits the store.

23RD
FLOOR

The Jekyll & Hyde Office Coordinator

1

You are surely familiar with the tale of *Dr. Jekyll and Mr. Hyde*? It is a story about split personalities to put it in the simplest terms.

In Rober Louis Stevenson's story, Dr. Jekyll needed a potion to change into Mr. Hyde.

Now, envision this alteration potion-free.

I knew a young woman who displayed unpredictable behavior; mean-spirited one moment, the next surprisingly sweet. Would you like to hear to hear the tale?

It was a Tuesday afternoon…

2

Rose Wright considered herself a management professional extraordinaire.

Calling her a secretary was a grave mistake. If you did, the *Wrath of Wright* would come down upon you.

"I am no secretary! Do you understand?" Rose would inform the little peon that brought it forth. "I'm an office coordinator. This place would burn down without me! Am I making myself clear?!"

The response from whomever was *crystal clear (dead silence)* as they retreated from the office to save themselves from further scolding.

"Good afternoon, Rose," I said to her as I came into the office. "How are you today?"

"Hello, Ross," she responded. "I am doing fine. Thank you for asking. I have everything set for your meeting. Tim will be along in a moment."

"Thanks, Rose," I responded.

As I went into Tim's office, one of our floor associates came into her office. The conversation that ensued was a kicker, making my point.

3

"Hello, Rose. How are you doing today?"

"Fine, Abigail. What can I do for you?"

"I seem to have lost my badge. I need you to issue me a new one so that I can punch in for my shift."

"You're joking, right?" Rose asked with a stern gaze fixed on her. "Again? Abigail, that is the third badge this week!"

"I know, I'm…"

"Sorry?" interrupted Rose. "You're not sorry, Abigail. You are downright irresponsible! Do you understand what kind of hassle it is to issue you, or anyone, with a new badge when they lose it? I must revise every punch."

"No, but…" Abigail tried to explain.

Rose interrupted her again. "But what? I must inform the corporate office, avoiding their questions. Then I need to explain things to Tim, Abigail. Be aware these badges are costly."

The phone rang.

Rose stopped her rant and answered the phone in the sweetest manner possible.

"Thank you for calling the Shoe Box. This is Rose. How may I help you today?"

Rose was silent as she listened to the customer's request. She responded, "Yes, sir. One moment, please, I'll connect you with that department."

Rose placed the call on hold. Pressing the intercom, she called, "Men's department, I have a customer service phone call holding for you on line one. Men's department, customer service phone call on line one."

Rose hung up the phone and reverted back to nasty.

"As for you, Abigail, I will issue you a new badge. Retrieve it during your break; don't misplace it. Lose this one and the next will cost you; AND I'll ensure you work free for that day. Do you understand me?" asked Rose.

"Yes," said Abigail, close to tears.

"Now get out and get to work! *My* work requires *my* attention. Wasting my time replacing your badge every time you lose it is not productive!"

Abigail removed herself from the office expeditiously.

4

All I could do was sit there. I listened, fighting laughter during the exchange; it wasn't easy.

Though not hilarious, it was amazing to witness Rose as a Jekyll and Hyde secretary, sorry office coordinator. There was no doubt about it. All I can say is I am glad that I never suffered her wrath during my tenure at the Shoe Box.

22ND
FLOOR

Germ O Phobia

It's spooky season in Salem, Massachusetts.

Witches, ghouls, ghosts, and goblins are enjoying life, which has returned to normal after Covid.

Normal, for most. Some are taking things to the extreme. Here's a prime example for you.

My wife and I are sitting in the Boston Burger Company having lunch before continuing our tour of Salem when a man and his girlfriend (maybe wife, it's difficult to tell with the thick latex gloves they are wearing) walk into the restaurant.

Even though they are together, they stand as far apart (literally six feet) as they can in the small lobby space of the restaurant.

Their attire is almost identical.

Heavy jeans tucked into some fancy western boots. Lightweight jackets duct taped around the wrists to prevent anything, including air, from getting up them, and of course those thick industrial-strength latex gloves. They both have on tight fitting skull caps, wear protective eyewear, and of course, those infamous masks! Not the cinch doctor's style masks. We're talking about the heavy duty N95 style nuclear masks strapped as tight to their faces as they can get them. Hazmat suits would've been the better option. This look may have scared some, but seems normal to others. But it's Halloween time in Salem, so they fit right in, and no one pays them any attention.

As the hostess walks up, she looks at them and jokingly states, "Let me guess… medical conference, right? Perhaps part of the Purge group that's in town?"

"Neither," says the man in a serious tone.

"Honey," snaps the woman in a raspy, snotty voice. "You are aware of the ongoing pandemic, right? Everyone in this establishment needs to be wearing a mask! Every one of you could kill us!"

"Seriously," replies the hostess in her thick Boston accent. "Sweety, pandemic's over. Life has gotten back to normal. Perhaps you and the wonder twin should lock yourselves up at home if you're that worried. Now, are you eating here or what?"

"Table for two," says the man. "As far away from anyone as possible."

"Yeah, that ain't gonna happen," responds the hostess.

As she escorts them into the dining area, they can see why. The dining space is tight and packed to maximum capacity. Tables are mere inches apart, while still providing ample space for patrons to move and eat with no inconvenience.

"Here you go," says the hostess, seating the couple right smack dab in the middle of the dining area.

The couple lacks enthusiasm.

Before they sit down, both reach into their jacket pockets and pull-out disinfecting wipes.

Removing a couple each, they synchronously wipe down the table and chairs thoroughly before sitting down.

Usually, people take their jackets off before sitting down. Not these two. They leave everything intact as they sit down. It's a nice fall day and warm enough to not need a jacket. Despite the air conditioning, it's warm in the restaurant because of the crowd. They must be sweating like crazy sitting there, yet it doesn't seem to bother them.

Their server brings over a menu for each of them to peruse, touching them as little as possible. After a few minutes, she returns to take their order and then they sit in silence and wait.

If the bizarre way they're dressed isn't enough fodder, when the food arrives, the real fun begins.

Instead of using the silverware the restaurant has provided, they each carry a set of disposable cutlery, sealed in a thick plastic package.

By this time, everyone in the restaurant is taking notice of them.

Despite the restaurant's noisy atmosphere, one can still overhear conversations and comments about the couple.

Watching them is quite a spectacle.

They take turns taking a bite or a drink. Everyone watches as they hold their breath, remove their mask, insert a bite or swallow, then replace their mask so that they can breathe while they finish chewing or swallowing, whichever the case may be.

The couple eat like it is their last meal either of them will have. Once they finish, the man calls for the check. He uses his credit card to pay the bill and when the server returns it to him, douses his gloves in hand sanitizer, gingerly picks up the card, pulls a disinfecting wipe out, then wipes down the card before placing it back in his wallet.

He pulls out another wipe and uses it to pick up the pen. He wipes it down before he signs the receipt. Prior to departing, they collect the used wipes in a small bag and leave it in the center of the table. They exit the restaurant, avoiding all interaction.

Once they are outside, they walk from view, being careful to stay six feet apart from one another. It is an amusing sight that gets a round of laughs and cheers from everyone inside as they watch them leave.

"Talk about taking things to the extreme," comments a patron to his server.

"They were paranoid, to say the least," responds the server.

"That's an understatement," I say to my wife, hearing the comment.

"I'd recommend professional help, but I don't think it will work," says my wife as we go back to planning the rest of our afternoon while finishing our lunch.

21ST
FLOOR

G.W.M.

1

It is a Saturday morning, a curious time to hold a meeting. Meetings often took place on Sunday nights after the store's closing. Pizza and pop (soda for you non-Michiganders) were always on the menu. Not today. Management didn't even have the common courtesy of bringing in coffee and donuts. Bastards!

"To what do I owe the pleasure of attending this meeting?" asks Phil, the men's department manager of the Shoe Box.

"Perhaps the pleasure is ours, Phil, watching you get your pink slip!" quips Janet, who manages the ladies' department.

"Cute," says Phil. "Regardless, who holds a meeting on a Saturday morning?"

"We've all been asking that," responds Jose, the stock lead. "This isn't something management can just disseminate to us at their convenience. Otherwise, why drag everyone in here?"

"You might have a point there, Jose," says Janet. "Who's the guy talking with Skippy and Paul?"

"No clue," says Phil. "Whoever it is has Skippy worried and they're walking this way, so I'd say we're about to find out."

2

Skippy, the general manager, walks over to address them.

"Good morning. Please take a seat so we can get started."

He waits a moment as the entire crew settles down.

They take longer than expected.

Skippy appears on edge and is about to burst.

Before he can, Andy, the assistant store manager (who should be the general manager), steps in.

"Okay, everyone. The sooner you settle, the sooner we can start, allowing non-workers to leave early and giving the rest of us a head start before the store opens."

With that being said, the crew becomes dead silent. You can tell who they respect and who they don't. The gentleman Skippy is about to introduce notices this and he's not impressed… and Skippy knows it.

"Thank you," says Skippy in a rude tone. "I called this meeting this morning to inform you there are changes being made in the company's structure. Effective today, we move into a new region because of the company's realignment of stores to be more efficient."

Skippy's hands shake as he takes a sip of his coffee and states, "We have a new regional manager…and I have a new boss. So, allow me to introduce you to our new regional manager, Gabriel W. McClellan."

3

Gabriel W. McClellan steps forward, revealing himself to the staff for the first time.

He is a weathered individual with a chiseled face resembling Gregory Peck, but he walks with a stagger that would rival John Wayne's. In his early fifties, the man looks all business and won't take shit from anyone.

That's the assumption everyone gets; one soon to become a proven fact.

"Good morning, everyone," says Gabriel. "Thank you for taking the time this morning to come to this meeting. It's appreciated. I felt it was best to speak to all of you to introduce myself initially. I will attempt to get to know each of you personally as we collaborate."

He takes a drag on his cigarette, sips his coffee, then continues with his speech.

"As Skippy said, my name is Gabriel W. McClellan and as of today, I am your new regional manager. My mother named me after the archangel Gabriel. Those familiar with the Bible, Gabriel, announced God's will to humanity. My mother will confirm that I did so on the day of my birth, hence my name."

The staff laughs at his statement.

"A comedian," comments Jose to Phil.

"You may call me G.W., as that is what I go by," explains Gabriel.

He informs the staff, "I have an extensive background in the shoe business and those at the corporate level, the Ivory Tower to you, have the utmost faith and confidence in my abilities to get the job done and accomplish the company's objectives."

"Well," whispers Phil to Jose, "I think Skippy is up a 'shit crick' with this guy."

"Ya think," responds Jose.

"Some of you here today," says G.W., "see this job as a stepping stone to something else. That's fine. While you're with this company, I expect you to do your job to the best of your ability."

He pauses, takes a sip of coffee and another drag off his cigarette.

"The rest of you who want to move up within the company, it's my job to give you all the tools and the knowledge needed for you to succeed in that goal."

G.W. takes one last drag off his cigarette and crushes it out in the ashtray sitting on the shelf next to him. He finishes his coffee and warns the staff in a serious tone, "I don't tolerate complainers! Want to complain? There's the door!" he states, pointing to the exit. "You are free to use it anytime! Complainers are a dime a dozen, and I'll replace you like that!" snapping his fingers. "Are we *clear*?"

The staff sits there, stunned.

Even Phil, who would've had some sarcastic remark, says *nothing*.

"Questions?" asks G.W.

No one says a word. Who would after that?

G.W. waits, then after no response, says, "Since there are no questions, you may go. Again, thank you for coming in. I look forward to working with all of you. Enjoy your day."

4

G.W. turns and walks away, with Skippy and Andy following him. His conversation with them doesn't look good based on both manager's body language.

"Well, that was fun," says Phil. "Let's do it again sometime."

"I'll pass, thank you very much," Janet comments as she gathers her things. "The time for a career change may have arrived."

"What do you think, Jose?"

"Well, Phil, I must admit it's an introduction that I will never forget. I'll reserve my opinion until I've worked with him. However, I think we are in for one interesting ride with one G.W. McClellan."

"Time will tell," says Phil as they disperse. "Time will tell."

20TH
FLOOR

60 Miles Per Hour Through
McDonald's Parking Lot

1

Sebastian wakes as his *Star Wars Talking Alarm Clock* goes off.

The beeps, tweets, chirps, and whistles of R2-D2 echo in the room. Then he hears the familiar voice of C-3PO speak out.

"What R2-D2 is saying is that you have to get up right away."

R2-D2 chirps out a series of beeps which C-3PO interprets…

"R2, you shouldn't be so polite. This little rebel is about to be late."

The final set of tweets and whistles from R2 leave 3PO to remind Sebastian…

"Don't forget to wind the clock so that we can wake you again tomorrow."

The clock then makes a series of clicking noises before repeating the message as Sebastian lies there and ignores it.

As the message repeats, his mother walks into the room to turn it off.

"It's time to get up, Sebastian," she tells him, opening the curtains to the morning sun. "The movers will arrive soon. I want you and your sister ready to go before they arrive."

"Why is it again that we are moving to Grand Rapids?" asks Sebastian.

"I've been through this with you, Sebastian," says his mother explaining the situation to him again for the umpteenth time, "I took a promotion so I can run a *Little Red Shoe House* store of my own. That store is down in Grand Rapids. Your father and I are divorcing, and northern Michigan isn't big enough for the two of us. Not to mention it will be a fresh start for everyone."

"So you say," says Sebastian.

"That I do. Now get your butt moving. I have some loose ends to address before the movers arrive."

Sebastian understands there's no sense in arguing with his mother. Once she's decided, there's no changing her mind. *It's time to move forward,* as she's told his sister and him multiple times over the last few weeks.

2

The *Belkins* moving truck backs into the two-track driveway at Sebastian's home on Jefferson Avenue in Petoskey, Michigan, at 9 a.m.

After coordinating with his mother, the moving team makes quick work of emptying the house.

Sebastian and his sister Linda watch as the rooms of the house get evacuated of their contents, leaving nothing but emptiness behind.

Even the basement, which seems scary many times, has lost its luster.

Between intervals of watching the movers do their job, Sebastian and Linda assist their mom loading the car with miscellaneous items the movers aren't taking.

Three hours later, the job is done.

With everything now loaded, the moving truck pulls out of the driveway and heads to Grand Rapids, Michigan, where it will be met by Sebastian, Linda, and his mom the next morning.

Sebastian's mom goes through the house one last time to make sure they took everything. She secures it and leaves the keys for the realtor in a designated spot for the new family. Prior to entering the car, they gather outside to gaze at the house one last time.

"So many memories we're leaving here, Mom," says Sebastian.

"Yes. We had a good run here though," she tells both of her children. "Now it's time to start a new chapter and make fresh memories. It's all a part of life."

Mom gets in the car and starts it as Linda climbs into the backseat. Sebastian picks up their dog Rooter and puts him in the car. He then gets in the passenger seat. He shuts the door and Mom pulls out of the driveway. After a momentary pause, she drives south to Reed City to spend the night with her parents.

3

Along the way, the family stops in Kalkaska, Michigan, for a bite to eat at *Big Boy*. Linda orders a cheeseburger and some fries. Mom has her favorite – a *Classic Big Boy* (nothing more than a fancy *Big Mac*). Sebastian orders a grilled cheese which he proceeds to douse in ketchup, a lot of ketchup. Ketchup is a food group. At least, according to Sebastian it is.

While they eat, Mom pulls out a folder that contains the floor plan to their new home in Grand Rapids. It's not a house, but an apartment in a complex called *Normandy East*. She explains who will get what bedroom and what amenities the complex offers.

"Wow! They have a pool we can use anytime!" exclaims Linda.

"Forget the pool," says Sebastian. "My room has its own bathroom!"

"We will also be close to a mall, movie theatres, and restaurants, some you've never even heard of," says their mother. "*Toys R Us* is also nearby," she adds, trying too hard to sell it.

"Sweet!" says Sebastian.

They finish their meal and continue their journey to Grandma's house in Reed City. Linda and Sebastian are eager to share all their exciting news with their grandparents once they get there.

Their Mom sits and listens to her children's enthusiasm. Perhaps not as bad as she initially thought.

4

Dinner that night is courtesy of Grandma and Grandpa who go down to the *Dairy Depot* and pick up hot dogs, fries, and huge chocolate malts to split between everyone one. Sebastian doesn't want to split the malt. He knows he can drink the whole thing on his own, but Grandma insists.

The next morning, Sebastian and Linda are up early, eager to depart for their new home.

"What's for breakfast?" asks Linda.

"We are going to stop at *McDonald's* in Big Rapids," says Grandma.

"That sounds good," says Sebastian.

Going to *McDonald's* is a rare treat.

Sebastian then asks, "You're coming with us?"

"Yes," says Grandma. "I told your mom I'd take a couple of days off and help you all settle in."

"So, who's riding with me?" asks Mom.

"I want to ride with Mom and Rooter," says Linda.

"That works," says Sebastian. "I'll ride with Grandma. I am her favorite, after all."

Sebastian's Grandma scolds him.

"Sebastian Gary!" his grandmother scolds him. You know you're in trouble when relatives use your middle name. "You realize I don't play favorites!" she informs him.

"Yes, you do," says my mom. "but that's a discussion for another time. Shall we hit the road?"

Everyone says their goodbyes to Grandpa, and they are on the way. Since grandma is clueless of where she's going, except as far a Big Rapids, she follows her daughter.

Sebastian and his grandmother discuss the move on the fifteen-minute drive down to Big Rapids. He expresses his excitement about moving, despite opposing it in the beginning.

Sebastian can see *McDonald's* ahead on the right-hand side of the road. He sees his mom turn on her turn signal and make the turn into the parking lot.

The events that unfold next astonish both Sebastian and his grandmother.

Once Mom is in the parking lot, she turns into a speed demon. Sebastian watches as she speeds up (zero to sixty in a second). Even with speed, she navigates the lot and parks on the restaurant's opposite side. The way she drives, Mom looks like she is trying to outrun a police officer hot on her tail.

A few seconds later, Grandma and Sebastian pull into the spot next to her.

Mom and Linda are already out of the car waiting as Grandma parks her car.

"Where's the fire, Chummy?" asks Grandma.

"What are you talking about?" asks Mom with an innocent look on her face.

"You must be starving, Mom," says Sebastian. "You were whipping through the parking lot like the *Bandit*!"

"I don't know what you think you saw, Sebastian, but I wasn't!" states his mom.

"Oh, yes you did, Mom," says Linda. "Let's do it again, except without Rooter. He's a little shook up from the incident."

"I don't know what you are talking about," says Mom, adding, "Or what it is you *think* you saw."

"Okay," says Grandma. She winks at both Sebastian and Linda and tells her daughter, "It's your story, Chummy."

"Yes, it is. Now let's get something to eat. We need to be in Grand Rapids no later than 10:30 a.m. and it's 8:45 a.m. now."

The debate is over as they head inside for breakfast, afterward continuing their journey to their new home.

5

The story you just read is true. Names, of course, changed to protect the innocent. To this day, it refuses to die as I and my sister have never let my mother forget it. What a way to start fresh memories. Mom speeding through *McDonald's* at sixty miles an hour!

19TH
FLOOR

Turning The Tide

1

Carley has had a long week. The week is done; the weekend is hers. Her boyfriend, Finny, also has the weekend off. He drove up to Reed City this morning as a surprise. Currently, he's in the kitchen, using his culinary talents to prepare a homemade spaghetti dinner. A candlelit spaghetti dinner, no less. A romantic evening is ahead. Her expectation is that it rivals the one out of *Walt Disney's Lady and the Tramp*.

As she sets the table, the phone rings. Placing the plates on the counter, she walks over to the doorway and answers the phone.

"Hello", says Carley as she listens to the person on the other end.

"Thank you, but I'm not interested."

Another moment of silence. "Again, I'm not interested," she tells the caller and hangs up the phone.

"What was that all about?" asks Finny

"Another idiot telemarketer trying to sell me something again! I've come home the past few nights and my answering machine has been full of messages from them."

"Then change your number."

"I've done that once. It's an expense I shouldn't need to incur because these telemarketers, even though I know they're just doing their jobs, continue to pester me."

"You'd think if they always get a machine, they'd make a notation and stop calling."

"I do so love your optimism, Finny. But give yourself a demerit for it! You and I both know they aren't that smart, and it won't happen."

"True. *You* need to relax. Finish setting the table as dinner is about ready," says Finny, giving her a kiss on the forehead.

2

The scene is ideal.

Candles provide a soft light in the room and on the table. The table has been perfectly set, and the food on it looks appetizing.

Carley turns on the stereo and puts on a nice romantic soundtrack, setting the volume to just the right level. Finny pours the wine. They take their seats and begin dishing their plates. Once they are both ready, Finny raises his glass.

"Here's to a…" starts Finny as the phone's ringing interrupts his sentence.

"Dammit!" says Carley.

"Ignore it," Finny tells her.

They wait a minute and the phone goes silent.

"You see," says Finny as he once again raises his glass. "As I was saying…"

Before he can utter another word, the phone interrupts him again.

"That's it!" says Carley. "I'm going to end this."

"How?" asks Finny.

"I'm going to answer this phone and have a bit of fun," she tells him. "Care to listen?"

"With that look you have in your eye, I can't wait to hear this one," he responds. "This should be good."

Finny goes to the living room phone while Carley answers the one in the kitchen.

"Now," she says as they simultaneously pick up the phones.

"Hello," says Carley.

3

"Do I have the pleasure of speaking with Miss Lang?" asks the caller.

"You do," responds Carley in a sultry voice.

"Miss Lang, my name is Stephen Huber, and I am with State Farm."

"State Farm?" she questions. "Then you deal with insurance," states Carley, sounding like she has a clue who he represents.

"That is correct, Miss Lang," responds Stephen.

"Oh, Stephen," coos Carley, being coy. "I already have insurance, both home and car. And please, call me Carley."

Finny realizes what Carley is up to. He thinks to himself, *This will be fun.*

"Miss Lang, I mean Carley, though you already have insurance, State Farm might get you a better rate than what you are paying now. We could save you some money in the long run by switching to us," explains Stephen.

"Stephen, that is such a gracious gesture," comments Carley. "Why don't we have dinner together and discuss it?" she proposes.

Silence is Carley's answer. It is clear she has thrown him off guard and now he's in uncharted waters.

"I'm sorry, Miss Lang. That's something I can't do," he tells her.

"Well, why not?" asks Carley. She explains, "It's obvious you want to sell me something. So take me out to dinner. That way, we can discuss the potential of what you're selling. Isn't that protocol for making a deal? You take your client(s) out to dinner and make your pitch?"

Stephen tries to get back to his original point. "Again, Miss Lang, I'm only asking you to listen to what we offer, compare it to what you have, and decide from there."

"Oh, so this is a bait and switch tactic. You don't want to sell me something you're only interested in getting into my pants! That's what you want, isn't it?"

Both Finny and Stephen didn't see this one coming. Finny is damn near on the floor in a laughing fit and poor Stephen is at a loss for words.

"Miss Lang, I…" says Stephen.

"Stephen, it's Carley," she says to him in a calm and sultry manner, "If you want to get into my pants, sweetheart, you need to wine and dine me. I don't give it up that easily. Do a good job and I may even take you up on your offer. When are you available?"

A clicking sound and the line goes dead.

As she hangs up the phone, Carley says to Finny, "Guess he wasn't interested. Oh, well."

"His loss," says Finny, rolling his eyes at her as he hangs up his phone. "Can't believe how you flipped the script on him out of nowhere."

"Guarantee you, it will be a call he won't soon forget," comments Carley.

"It won't be one I'll forget," says Finny. "Bet you he is still dumbfounded, sitting there at his desk trying to figure out how things went catty wampus so quick. I don't think he will make the mistake and call again."

"Probably not," agrees Carley. "Now where were we?"

18TH
FLOOR

Hello, Fat Boy!

1

The phone rings.

Before I can even get to it, my mother has answered it upstairs in the kitchen. After a moment, she yells down to my bedroom, "Royce, your friend Kevin is on the phone for you."

I get up from my desk, where I'm reading a Jack L. Chalker novel, walk over to the nightstand where the phone is, and pick up the receiver. I yell back, "Got it, Ma!"

When I hear the click as she hangs up the other, I begin my conversation with Kevin. "Speak," I say.

"WOOF!" responds Kevin. "You know, son, you really need to cut down your intake of movie dialogue. Come up with something original."

"Yeah, like that's going to happen. So, what's up?" I ask.

"Just curious what you are up to?" responds Kevin.

"I am reading the third book to the Jack L. Chalker series you got me hooked on."

"Told you it would. How far in are you?"

"About halfway."

"Well, I won't spoil it for you. The upcoming event sets the stage for the superior last book! All hell's about to break loose! When the main character starts…"

"Enough already," I say, cutting him off. "I'm good with some spoilers, but I'm already intrigued as it is. Do me a favor. Shut the fuck up!"

"Royce, assume that I *will* spoil it for you at some point," says Kevin.

"Of *that*, I have no doubt. So I better become a speed reader before you do. Anyway, what's up?"

"Well," says Kevin, "I need to get a birthday gift for my brother. My mom's throwing him a surprise birthday party this weekend and I thought since I was going out that you might want to tag along."

"A trip to *Toys R Us*, is it?"

"Indeed."

"You know me too well, my friend. I never decline this type of opportunity. Hold on a sec and I'll check to see if it's okay," says Royce.

Royce puts the phone down and yells upstairs, "Hey, Mom!"

"Yes, Royce," she answers.

"Kevin needs to get a birthday gift for his brother. He wonders if I can tag along."

"Is your homework done?"

"Yes. Isn't it always? You're confusing me with my sister. She's the one you need to worry about with homework."

"Don't get snarky! You can go. Be back by 9:30, though."

"Thanks, Mom!" says Royce, going back to the phone.

He picks up the receiver and tells Kevin, "No problem. When will you be over?"

"I'll be there in twenty," says Kevin.

"Sounds good, my friend. I'll see you then," says Royce as he hangs up the phone.

2

45 minutes later.

Royce sees Kevin coming down the street. If he hadn't seen him, he would have heard him coming because Kevin is blaring the car stereo with the latest Pat Benatar cassette. He grabs his coat and yells to his mom, "Okay, Mom. I'll be back later. Love you!"

"Sounds good. You guys behave yourselves. Love you too," she replies.

Royce heads out the back door. He walks on the sidewalk beside the house to the driveway as Kevin pulls in.

He opens the passenger door and Kevin turns down the volume on the stereo as he gets in. "Twenty minutes, huh? Try more like forty-five," says Royce as he shuts the door.

"It was twenty minutes," retorts Kevin. "Twenty minutes by my time."

"Oh, yes, I forgot, oh great one. There is standard time. Then there is Kevin Foley time. You, sir, are going to be late to your own funeral. You realize that, don't you?"

"Of course I do! The reaper can adjust to my time, just like everyone else."

"That ought to piss him off!"

"Exactly," comments Kevin as he pulls out of the driveway and heads down the street. "So, which *We B Toys* should we go to?"

"Depends on what you are looking for. What's he into?" asks Royce.

"He is totally in love with that show *Dinosaurs*. Otherwise, anything *Transformers*, *G.I. Joe*, or *Masters Of The Universe* related will work as well," says Kevin.

"Head towards the 28th Street store. They have a better selection of figures than the Alpine one. If they don't have what you want *Dinosaurs* related, they'll have plenty of the others to choose from."

"28th Street it is, my friend," says Kevin, heading in that direction. "Knew there was a reason I had you tag along."

3

Royce and Kevin chat along the way as they make the fifteen-minute drive across town from the north end of Grand Rapids.

Multiple times during the trip, Kevin attempts to spoil the *Four Lords Of The Diamond* series that he hooked Royce on. He's shot down every time, the final one as they pull into the parking lot of *Toys R Us*.

As they exit, Kevin says in defeat, "Fine. Let's stay focused on the birthday gift."

They walk across the parking lot to a flight of steps, bordered by a handicap ramp, leading up to the store's entrance. As they reach the doors, the sensors trigger, and they open into a vestibule that is filled with many blue shopping carts bearing the store's logo. Passing the carts, they trigger a second set of doors and walk into the store.

The rush of air hits them as the doors open, and the smell of new toys hits their nostrils.

"Ahh," says Kevin. "I so love the aroma of a good toy store in the morning! There's nothing quite like it!"

They look down the vast aisles filled with toys for every interest. If Toys R Us doesn't have it, chances are you will not find it.

"Figures are in the back aisles. I'm guessing the *Dinosaurs* items are nearby. So, I'd start there," suggests Royce.

"Lead the way, my friend," says Kevin.

Royce and Kevin make their way through the store towards the back aisles. They pass through the aisles of *Legos*, of course, and the aisle of video games with an excellent selection of from *Atari, Intelevison,* and *Coleco-Vision.*

Royce cuts down the stuffed animal aisle.

Halfway down, he notices the perfect gift for Kevin's brother… an official *Disney/Henson Dinosaurs* Baby Sinclair.

Baby Sinclair is plush and has a pull string. With each pull of the string, he speaks his catch phrases from the show using Kevin Clash's voice to a tee.

"Talk about too easy," says Royce. "Your brother is what, like three? This, my friend, will be perfect," says Royce as he picks one up from the shelf.

He pulls the cord.

"I'M THE BABY, GOT TO LOVE ME."

Royce pulls it a second time.

"NOT THE MOMMA!"

"The signature phrase," says Royce. "I'd go with this and it's only $20. That's not too bad."

Kevin agrees with Royce but, of course, wants to try it for himself. He pulls the cord and the toy replies…

"HELLO, FAT BOY!"

Royce busts out laughing. Yes, not nice, but Kevin is oversized. He isn't fat, just pleasantly plump.

"Why are you laughing?" asks Kevin.

"I can't help but laugh. It's like the thing knows. Even though that's how he talks to his father, Earl, on the show. It is one of his signature phrases. Try it again," says Royce.

Kevin reluctantly agrees with Royce's assessment. He pulls the cord again and the toy sputters…

"HELLO, FAT BOY!"

"I think it's broken," says Kevin.

"Give it here," says Royce and he pulls the cord again. The toy says…

"AGAIN!"

Just to show Kevin that it isn't broken and is simply a fluke, he pulls the cord again. This time the toy states…

"NOT THE MOMMA!"

"You see," says Royce. "Works just fine. It's possible that the toy might repeat from time to time. Though the idea is for the toy to cycle through its sayings."

It does not convince Kevin. So he pulls another one from the shelf and tries it.

"HELLO, FAT BOY!"

Royce is beside himself. "Here, get take this one," handing the plush toy to Kevin.

Kevin tries the new one. Again, the same result.

Frustrated, Kevin rummages through the shelf trying each Baby Sinclair he can find. Each one he tries, no matter how many times he pulls the pull string with each; the phrase is always…

"HELLO, FAT BOY!"

Kevin throws up his hands in defeat. "Well, that was a good idea, Royce. Let's search for something else. I hate this damn thing!"

"I think it's you," says Royce as he picks another up and holds it towards Kevin. He pulls the cord twice, and it says…

"HELLO, FAT BOY! I'M THE BABY, GOT TO LOVE ME."

"With that, my friend, I rest my case," says Kevin as he storms out of the aisle to look for something else.

17TH
FLOOR

The Day The Golden Mic
Went Silent

1

February 17, 2021, started out like any other Wednesday.

Being Wednesday meant it was writing day. I call them Writing Wednesdays. My dedicated day where from 9 a.m. to 3 p.m. you will find me in my office working on my next novel or novels depending on the day.

On that Wednesday, for what reason I can't recall, I took a break. I ran up to the local quick stop, put gas in the car, grabbed a lottery ticket (that didn't win…typical), and picked up a pop (soda for those non-Michiganders). I paid and returned to my car.

As I started the car, the familiar riff of The Pretenders's song *My City Is Gone* blared through the speakers. It was seven minutes past noon and that music could mean only one thing… *The Rush Limbaugh Show* and three hours of *"Broadcast Excellence"*, as Rush so eloquently put it each day, was about to begin.

I wondered whether Rush's distinct voice would open the show (he'd been off for some time dealing with health issues). In Rush's absence, a guest host chosen by Rush stepped in as the music reached its cue.

When the music reached its cue, the voice coming over the radio was not the one I, nor anyone else listening on that day, had expected.

2

The voice was none other than Kathryn Adams Limbaugh, Rush's beloved wife.

As Kathryn spoke, you could tell she was a natural. *This is going to be a real treat today*, I thought, Rush's wife hosting the program.

Then the tone of her voice shifted after her initial greeting.

She told everyone, *"I am not the Limbaugh you tuned in to listen to."*

In an instant, my heart sank. Gut instinct told me Kathryn's next words would not be good.

I wanted to be wrong.

However, that would not be the case. She told the audience, and I quote…

"It is with profound sadness I must share with you directly that our beloved Rush… passed away this morning due to complications from lung cancer."

3

I sat there stupefied; tears welled up in my eyes.

Ever had that befuddled sensation you get when you receive news that a family member, close loved one, or a dear friend has passed away? If you have, then you grasp my emotions.

I'd gone numb.

I asked myself, *Why was I experiencing this over a celebrity?*

It's not as if I knew Rush personally. I never spoke or corresponded with him. Hell, I never even met the man. My only interaction with Rush was during the hours of noon and three, Monday through Friday, during his broadcasts since the early 1990s.

I listened to Rush daily and rarely missed a day.

Most days, I could only listen for a bit (work interfered). Some Rush was better than no Rush. On those days, I read the daily email with the show's highlights. On my days off or during vacation, I tried my best to tune in for the entire three hours.

You may not have liked or agreed with Rush, but he loved this country. In today's world, that's becoming a rarity. In his words, *Don't doubt me.* Need proof? Pick up one of his *Rush Revere* history books or one of the other books that he wrote. You can tell from his writing how much he loved his country and its rich history.

Rush inspired me, and he had a simple theory.

Everyone has the potential to accomplish anything in our great country.

You succeed by investing your mind, heart, and soul into your goal. By putting all your efforts and your God-given talents into it, not panicking, and never giving up, you will persevere. If you need any evidence of this, read or listen to his many monologues, speeches, and interviews that he gave. They tell the tale.

Even though I never met Rush, I have known the man indirectly for nearly thirty years. Rush always said he had *"Talent on loan from…GOD!"* during each broadcast that he did. But on this date, February 17, 2021, that *talent* returned to God, the day the golden mic carrying his voice to all of us went silent.

16TH
FLOOR

The After Thought

1

Ted Barrington walks into the reception area of the office of Dr. Hans Mueller, Doctor of Psychology.

He walks up to the desk and checks in while flirting with the receptionist, think young Molly Ringwald. Ted sits down and before he can get comfortable, Dr. Mueller sticks his head out of his office door and calls, "Ted Barrington."

"Yes," answers Ted.

"Come on back, Mr. Barrington, and let's talk for a while," says Dr. Mueller, escorting him in. He closes the door and asks, "Can I offer you any refreshment, sir?"

"A stiff drink would be nice," replies Ted.

"I'm sorry, Mr. Barrington. I'm afraid we have nothing like that here. Just coffee or water."

"How about a bullet, then?" remarks Ted as he looks around the plush office.

"Bullet, Mr. Barrington? Are you referring to one for a gun?" asks Dr. Mueller.

"Is there any other kind?" retorts Ted.

"Mr. Barrington," says Dr. Mueller in a serious tone, "When someone asks for a bullet, in my experience, they have a death wish. Do I need to consider you suicidal?"

"Suicidal? Come on, Doc, that's for amateurs. Not to mention I don't believe in it. So relax. I'll take that cup of coffee, though."

Dr. Mueller pours Ted a fresh cup of the best French roast coffee. As he hands it to him, he motions for Ted to have a seat.

Ted accepts the coffee and takes a sip as he sits down. "That's damn excellent coffee, Doc."

"Thank you, Mr. Barrington," says Dr. Mueller as he sits in the chair across from him.

"Shall we begin?" says Dr. Mueller as he pulls out a pad and pen from the side of his chair to take notes as they converse.

"Guess it's now or never," says Ted.

"I must say, Mr. Barrington, you are quite the interesting individual with a parched and sarcastic sense of humor," observes Dr. Mueller.

"Thank you… I think," says Ted as he takes a sip of his coffee, "And please, call me Ted. Mr. Barrington sounds way too formal."

"Of course, Ted," responds Dr. Mueller. "I'm here to make you feel comfortable so that we can talk about what's troubling you."

"Suppose the next question to come is for you to say something like *tell me about your childhood*," says Ted, attempting his best Freudian impersonation.

"Is your childhood relevant to the issue you came to see me about today?" asks Dr. Mueller.

"No," responds Ted. It's always the first question in movies when someone talks to a shrink.

"I prefer the term psychologist, Ted, and since I want us to be honest with one another, what you see in the movies is, well… fiction. This is *not* fiction. It's reality. So, if it applies to your issue, then I ask that you please share because it will better assist me in helping you. So, I will ask again. Is it relevant?"

2

"Germane?" asks Ted, switching the doctor's words with one that means the same. "I am nothing more than an afterthought, which is what's relevant. It's as simple as that."

"Interesting," says Dr. Mueller. "An afterthought, to whom, may I ask?"

"Whom?" questions Ted. "Where would you like me to start? Father? Sister? My wife, niece. I could bore you with a never-ending list. No matter how you slice it, not one of them gives a tinker's damn whether I'm around. I could drop dead, right here, right now, and when you inform them, I guarantee none of them will bat an eyelash or even shed so much as a tear… and I mean *none* of them!"

"I see," responds Dr. Mueller. "What about your mother?"

"What about her?" asks Ted.

"You failed to mention her in your opening rant."

"That's because she's taking a dirt nap, Doc."

"I am sorry for your loss and meant no offense for bringing it up."

"Thank you, Doc. None taken, you couldn't have known. It's possible that a significant part of this is because of her death."

"How's that in your view?"

"She was the foundation of the family. The compass that kept everyone on the right path. Her upbringing instilled in her the belief that family was essential. You could lose everything, but if you had your family, you were golden and were the richest person on the Earth. When she unexpectedly bought the farm, even though some of the best doctors in the country had just given her a clean bill of health, the family fell into chaos. They ignored what it meant to be family, lost their moral compasses, and all hell broke loose."

"What time frame did this all happen in?" asks Dr. Mueller.

"Maybe six months after she died would be my best guess. I can't tell you what happened following her death. I lost at least three, perhaps four, months of my life. You can talk to my wife. She can fill in that time gap for you. All I know is this. They all turned on me."

"Why do you think that is?"

"Well, Herr Doctor, it's rather simple… families fight over possessions," says Ted.

He explains, "When mom died, her will was crystal clear. It spelled out what everyone was to receive. However, certain family members disputed mom's wishes."

"I assume you were receiving some inheritance they assumed belonged to them?" asks Dr. Mueller.

"Bingo!" says Ted. "Give that man a prize. I sold the item without offering it to any of them beforehand. That did them in. I didn't give them any proceeds, which they felt entitled to."

"So, this really triggered them and from that point on, you were public enemy number one?"

"Give that man another prize!" exclaims Ted. "You are on it, aren't you, Doc?"

"What transpired after all of this?" inquires Dr. Mueller.

"Ostracization," answers Ted.

He explains, "The family held holiday gatherings as they always had. They made sure not to include me. My sister got married. I received no invitation. Father made accusations I was taking advantage of other family members and saying things I never said."

"I see," says Dr. Mueller as he jots down some notes on his pad.

"I may be a lot of things, Doc. An attitude… I've got one. On this, there is no debate. I can be downright mean or as sweet as a piece of candy. If desired, I can embody the chilling darkness of winter and the sinister nature of the Devil. I can be loyal as a dog, almost to a fault, I might add. It all depends on you and how you treat me," explains Ted.

"Sounds like they chose poorly from what I am gathering."

"You got that right," says Ted as he takes a drink of his coffee.

"You mentioned your wife earlier," says Dr. Mueller. He points out to Ted, "It's obvious she doesn't fit into the family drama. What makes you assume you're an afterthought to her?"

"First, she's soon to be my ex-wife for what I will call irreconcilable differences to keep it simple. Second, to her I am nothing more than a second-class citizen in my home. In marriage, partners support one another. Isn't that how it's supposed to work?"

"Yes, it's how it should work," admits Dr. Mueller.

"Well 99.9% of the time it is always her way or the highway, especially with her children from her previous marriage. Don't get me wrong, I understand standing by your kids through thick and thin, but in a choice between supporting your spouse or your kid, I'm on the losing end. I'm there only for my contribution to the household expenses. Anything else, an afterthought," explains Ted.

"What about your niece? Grandparents? How do they fit in?" asks Dr. Mueller.

"My grandparents, all of them were the best. They're rolling over in their graves right now, I'm sure, over all of this," says Ted. "As for my niece, I'm good when she needs something. Otherwise, she has her own life and is closer to her husband's family than she is to her own. No one hears anything from her. So to her, I am an afterthought."

Dr. Mueller sits silent for a couple of minutes as he jots down more notes about the conversation.

After what Ted considers is too long of a silence, he asks, "Hey, Doc. Thoughts?"

<h2 style="text-align:center">3</h2>

Dr. Mueller jots down one last note and then looks up from the pad to address Ted.

"Ted, have you ever considered this is your family's way of coping with the situation? I will wager that you are much like your mother, and you embody her spirit and all that she stood for. So, because they are upset and can't take it out on her as she is gone, you, my friend, are the scapegoat," explains Dr. Mueller.

He takes a sip of water and continues his explanation.

"Your niece wanted nothing to do with the situation. So, she just cut everyone off."

"And what about my soon-to-be ex-wife?" interrupts Ted.

"You failed to notice certain details within the relationship, especially those with the children from her previous relationship," explains Dr. Mueller.

Ted sits there speechless as he listens to this shrink's opinion. He becomes clearly agitated by it. "You're joking, right? This is your *expert* opinion?"

"Based on what I've heard during our session, yes," answers Dr. Mueller.

"Got that bullet I ask you for earlier, Doc?" asks Ted.

Coming up again, the question surprises Dr. Mueller. "I understood you didn't believe in suicide. That it was for amateurs," retorts Dr. Mueller.

"That I did, Doc. Never mind though. I have one here," says Ted as he pulls one out of his jacket pocket. "There's no need to worry. The bullet is not for me... it's for you."

"For me?" asks Dr. Mueller, looking perplexed. "You're going to give me a bullet?"

"I'm not just going to give you a bullet, Doc. I aim to put it in ya," says Ted.

"With what," asks Dr. Mueller.

"With this," says Ted, reaching behind him under his jacket and pulling out a .44 Magnum.

Dr. Mueller breaks into a cold sweat as he watches Ted meticulously loads the bullet into the gun's chamber. In this situation, Dr. Mueller asks the typical question seen in the movies: "Why?"

"It's elementary, Herr Doctor. You assume you have all the answers. You know everything when, in fact, you know nada! Doctors don't listen to their patients and don't pay attention to the smallest of details which costs lives in the long term. If your kind did, everyone would be better off," explains Ted.

"Since you *assume* I missed something, and you seem to know more than I do, tell me what it is," says Dr. Mueller, now defiant in the situation he finds himself in.

"Well, Doc," says Ted as he gets up to lean in. "It's rather simple. You say it's their way of dealing with things. That's a crock! It's simple human nature in my book. My family hates me. You decipher their motives. My father never wanted kids. He so much as told me so during a recent argument. Everyone treated my sister like royalty, and she developed a superiority complex. My niece, just self-centered. My ex-wife understood the concept of family, but not the commitment of marriage. Regardless, their actions lead to one thing for me. I. AM. AN. AFTERTHOUGT!"

Ted cocks the gun, informing Dr. Mueller, "Now, so are you."

15TH
FLOOR

We Would Be Honored If You Would Join Us

1

"You have one minute before the start of your lunch break, Mr. Dyer," announces Theo. "Please finish your current thought before disconnecting from the system and shutting down for your break."

"I am aware of the time, Theo. Thank you anyway," responds Gordie with indifference still focusing on his writing.

Theo is Colony's Artificial Intelligence.

The Alignment designed it to keep all the employees on schedule. It doesn't understand the type of person Gordie is. He works until the last possible second.

Efficient with no wasted time, an attribute Colony admires in their employees and impresses upon everyone else.

Gordie finishes his train of thought, then disconnects from the system. As he removes his headset, he quickly and methodically inspects his writing to ensure that no little "glitches" found their way into the writing like the one earlier.

There are none.

Gordie is impressed with his efforts to make up the ground lost during the glitch. When finished, it looks like it never happened. Breathing a sigh of relief, Gordie has more confidence than before that his superiors won't be asking questions about said glitch.

Gordie stows the headset, shuts down, and goes to lunch.

2

Lunch is a simply fifteen minutes, more than adequate, especially today. Today, the furthest thing from Gordie's mind is getting something to eat. He is more interested in the personal time that follows. Since this is the focus of his attention, Gordie grabs a quick bite, inhaling it on his way down to Colony's Archives.

The Archives contain everything the Alignment wants you to know.

Gordie's interest in Colony's Archives is specific… the speeches and lectures of Black Haven's founder and architect, Daniel Reinhardt.

There's nothing like a good philosophical speech with principles and ideals that you agree with to set your mind back into its proper frame.

Gordie walks into a small room a few feet inside the Archives' main hall. Entering, he walks down a small flight of stairs angled because of the small lecture hall setup. Sitting down in the primary seat of the room, Gordie cues up a specific list of speeches given by Mr. Reinhardt. Scanning through them, he quickly finds the one he is looking for and engages it.

The room goes dark. That's funny, Gordie thinks to himself. Usually, the lights just dim. Before he can address the problem, the lights come up. A holographic projection, one so perfect, that it looks like the real founder of the Alignment, Daniel Reinhardt, is right there in front of him giving his speech.

"Good afternoon. I am Daniel Reinhardt, and I am here today to share a vision. A vision that will save our society. One that will make us more efficient, free us from the infections of those insidious Neanderthals, the Auer Hammers.

The Auer Hammers are not part of us. They cannot fathom the beauty and fulfillment of the world we've created. No, they are what is wrong with our society - with their fantasies, their childish behavior, their weak reliance on… the arts. They encompass the very heart of what is truly wrong with our society of old.

*My vision refocuses us. Brings us out of disarray and
anarchy. Organizes us. We can give our people, our friends,
and our children focus and a future without distractions
and weakness that has pilfered the lives of those who
preceded us."*

Gordie listens intently as his mind relishes every word that Mr. Reinhardt speaks. He seems connected to the man. It's just what the doctor ordered. Gordie's mind and his thoughts get back on track. He feels like his old self once again. The one everyone knows.

Caught up in Mr. Reinhardt's words, Gordie loses all sense of time. He doesn't realize this until the hologram of Mr. Reinhardt states:

*"Gordie. I would get going. Otherwise, you'll be late for the
start of your afternoon. We wouldn't want that now.
Would we?"*

Gordie checks the time and realizes Mr. Reinhardt is correct. He has less than two minutes to get back before his afternoon agenda starts. Without hesitation, Gordie runs out of the Archives and back to his office. He forgets to shut down the hologram.

"You are very welcome, Mr. Dyer," says Daniel Reinhardt in an intriguing voice. "Fitz, if you would please."

Fitz Dominic steps out of the shadows and turns off the hologram. Instead of the hologram dissipating, it remains.

"Your assessment, Mr. Reinhardt?" asks Fitz.

"Oh, yes. He is the one we have been looking for. He will make a perfect addition to the Alignment. You have done well, Fitz, and are to be commended."

"Thank you, sir. Shall I set the meeting?"

"Yes. It needs to be done expeditiously. We *can't* afford to wait," infers Daniel Reinhardt.

3

The rest of Gordie's day goes by without a hitch; he works at optimal capacity. He feels like his old self again. Gordie is proud of himself and how he recovered from earlier in the day. On his way home, he treats himself to a very fancy dinner and beverage. After enjoying the delicious meal, he returns home for a quiet and restful evening.

4

The next morning, Gordie follows his routine to a tee. It is his typical daily routine like every other until he arrives at Colony. When he checks in with the retinal scanner, the schedule that prints out looks nothing like what he is used to seeing. Instead of having his whole day laid out before him, it lists but one item. Looking it over, it reads…

```
ITINERARY: GORDIE DYER
Wednesday, July 18, 2525

8:00am—8:05am:
Meeting with Mr. Dominic
```

Giving it another glimpse, Gordie figures out exactly what is going on. "Fuck me to tears!" he exclaims softly, shaking his head in disgust. "They found out! Now they'll be showing me the door, shiny new pink slip in hand! Isn't that just wonderful."

Gordie heads directly to Mr. Dominic's office… no reason to delay the inevitable.

Upon arriving, he stops briefly to compose himself into his usual demeanor, then walks in. He half expects Fitz to eighty-six him. However, just like any other morning, Fitz doesn't look up from his computer.

"Good morning, Mr. Dyer," he says and pauses, adding to the tension of the situation before asking, "And what is today's plan?"

"That would be the correct question, Mr. Dominic. I seem to only have one item on my agenda today. Advise me on what is happening next."

"Ahh, yes!" Fitz says, smiling with *"a cat that ate the canary"* expression. Turning his attention to Gordie, "It's your lucky day."

"I'm fired. That's how I'm lucky, right?" responds Gordie.

"Oh, quite the contrary, Mr. Dyer. You, my friend, are being accorded a very special invitation."

"A special invitation?" questions Gordie. "From whom might this invitation be, and for what, if I may ask, sir?"

"I'm sorry, Mr. Dyer. I am not at liberty to answer and discuss such questions," is Fitz's political response. "Your direction is to meet with your team at 8:10am. Ensure they are on track to meet the deadlines that we've discussed. You also need to cut that little wretched worm on the team, Mr. Hunter. He's pulling a Foley and needs to be made an example of. Then, after your meeting, report to Meeting Room 1355. Be there at 8:30am sharp. Depending on the outcome, the rest of your day will be determined. Clear?"

"Crystal, sir."

"That's all," says Fitz, returning his attention back to his computer.

Gordie exits the room at precisely 8:04am.

At 8:10am, he meets with his team and stresses the importance of staying on schedule to meet the imposed deadline. Gordie unscrupulously dismisses Mr. Zachary Hunter, making a firm example of him in front of everyone. "If you want to play a Foley, this is the result," explains Gordie.

A couple of minutes later, at 8:25am, he dismisses them to carry out their tasks.

Gordie then heads directly for Meeting Room 1355 to discover his fate. Though he is nervous about the situation, he is also extremely curious. The possibilities rattle around in his mind as he arrives at the meeting room. If he isn't being canned, what is his fate? As he enters the room, he'll find out.

5

A shaft of light illuminates a single chair at the rear end of the table. The remaining chairs are empty, except for the chair at the opposite end from Gordie. A figure is sitting there, shrouded in the shadows. *Who is it?* wonders Gordie.

"Sit down, Mr. Dyer," says a familiar voice from the shadow. "Make yourself comfortable."

"Thank you, sir," responded Gordie, taking the seat. Sitting in the shaft of light makes him feel like he is in an interrogation chamber, about to be grilled.

He learns differently as the Man in the Shadow speaks. "Mr. Dyer, or may I call you Gordie?" he asks.

"Gordie, by all means, sir."

"Gordie, I am impressed with you and your work here at Colony."

"Thank you, sir," responds Gordie.

"You are a dedicated model employee here at Colony. Damn near close too perfect. Too close, I might add. Never off schedule. You spend most of your time working up to the last moments. Efficient. If I didn't know any better, I'd assume you are a form of artificial intelligence… but you and I both realize you're not. Damn close, though. Now you had a slight setback, a hiccup, shall we say yesterday, did you not?"

Gordie isn't exactly sure how to respond at first. He decides no matter what, he will just speak the truth of it, answering, "Yes, sir. I did."

"What happened, may I ask?" inquires the Man in the Shadows.

"Sir, I have not been myself as of late. I've not been sleeping and while I was writing yesterday, I… got too vivid. Almost, and I hesitate to even want to use let alone say the word," he pauses, trying to force back a sudden urge to hurl, "*Artsy,*" he finishes, not believing the word just came out of his mouth. Recomposing himself quickly, he asserts, "Instead of being technical. I'm not sure what happened. There is no excuse for it. I believe I have corrected the issue and am back on track," Gordie tells him honestly.

"Indeed, you did" the Shadowed Figure agrees. You went to the Archives and pulled up an inspiring speech. This speech promoted the recalibration and rebooting of yourself and your mind. Thus, allowing you to get back on track.

"How can you know that, if I may ask?" inquires Gordie. No one saw what he did.

"Simple, Gordie. I was there and saw it firsthand," admits the Man in the Shadows. "Lights!"

The room illuminates, revealing none other than Daniel Reinhardt, leader of the Alignment.

Stunned by this turn of events, Gordie says, "Mr. Reinhardt… it is an honor."

"The honor is mine, Gordie," responds Daniel Reinhardt, giving Gordie a moment to adjust to the situation.

Daniel Reinhardt gets up from his seat and makes his way slowly around the table to Gordie. Reinhardt explains, "Gordie, what you did is a disgrace. Not only to yourself, but to society. Knowing what's at stake, you allowed yourself to lose control. One cannot do that for a second. We have ingrained the vividness of Art and its concept in our genes for centuries. It is our society's ultimate undoing. My vision, along with the formation of the Alignment, saved our society. We've come far, my friend. I won't bore you with the details that you are, I'm sure, fully aware of. We now stand on the precipice of where our society is. The stage where we purge *art* from our genes and future generations will no longer have to endure it. Ours is the last generation where it still creeps up. Most succumb to it, allow it to retake them and revert them back to the ways of before. We know them as the Besanko's. They are scum of society. An infestation in the Underground. But I digress. You, Gordie… you didn't succumb! You knew how to combat it so it wouldn't take you over. Excellent! The Alignment needs people like you helping society fight this. Teaching them how to recover, and to move on."

Gordie sits there, speechless.

Not wanting to sound stupid to such an intelligent man, Gordie gathers his thoughts before he speaks. "You're saying only a few have achieved what I did?"

"Correct. Very few Gordie," reiterates Daniel Reinhardt. He adds, "And those are the ones that belong with us!"

"With us?" questions Gordie.

"Yes, with us, Gordie," Daniel Reinhardt responds, motioning to himself. "With the Alignment," he clarifies. "Your impeccable work record, along with how you handled yourself with your minor hiccup, has not only saved you, but has presented you with a very rare opportunity. Only a fool would not accept it."

"What is it you are asking, Mr. Reinhardt?" asks Gordie, not wanting to assume.

"Come now, Gordie. You know what I am asking without me having to ask it now, don't you?"

"Yes, sir," responds Gordie, trying to contain his excitement.

"Don't be shy. State it, my friend."

"You are asking me to join you, join the Alignment. Be a part of the hierarchy that continues its goal of bringing this society to pure perfection."

"Spoken like a loyal member. Do you accept?" extending his hand to Gordie.

Getting up from his chair, as it is now appropriate, Gordie clasps Daniel Reinhardt's hand, shakes it, and states, "Mr. Reinhardt, it would be an honor."

"Welcome, my friend. I look forward to working with you."

Pride fills Gordie. He has only dreamed of this. Maybe that dream was about this. He will not dwell on it. Things happen because you work for them. He worked hard and now he is reaping the rewards and becoming a member of the elite.

Composing himself, Gordie asks, "When would you like me to start, Mr. Reinhardt?"

"You'll report to us this Thursday." responds Mr. Reinhardt. "Take the rest of today to acclimate yourself with your new apartment and all its luxuries. It is in the same building as our headquarters. Only the best."

"Thank you, sir. And efficient, I might add."

"Indeed. I've had your belongings moved there for you. As for your office, it will be ready for you on Thursday. Be there at 8am sharp. You'll spend Thursday bringing yourself up to speed on our work, and on your first case, which you will deal with on Friday. It is a building inspection for one Stephanie Pacelli. She's doing renovations on a house in an area we really haven't focused on before. It's time we bring that area of the city into conformity with the rest of Black Haven."

"I agree, sir. Parts of the city still need it. While we do it, we can rid ourselves of the vermin in the Underground simultaneously. I look forward to the challenge, sir," says Gordie.

Mr. Reinhardt shakes Gordie's hand once again, then tells him, "Now, if you'll excuse me, I have other issues that need my attention. And you, my friend, have your own items to take care of. We'll speak again Thursday afternoon, 4 pm sharp, in your office."

"Thank you, Mr. Reinhardt."

Gordie watches as Mr. Reinhardt departs the room.

As the door to Meeting Room 1355 closes, Gordie falls back into his seat. He simply sits there, coming to terms with what has just transpired. A member of the Alignment. An opportunity to aid in bringing Black Haven to pure perfection, as envisioned by Daniel Reinhardt. He relishes the challenge that lies before him. Gordie doesn't understand that his good fortune will lead him to a greater understanding of the Alignment.

Who and what they really are.

14TH
FLOOR

The Corner Of Indecision

1

I come upon a corner. A corner of indecision.

A four corner stop in the middle of nowhere. Why a four corner stop here? I wonder. Which way should I go?

Four possibilities, none of them revealing the correct path. So I sit and ponder which direction will be best.

The obvious choice… turn around. Trace back my steps to regain the GPS signal and navigate to my intended location.

That is the easy way.

This approach may prove unsuitable.

What lies behind me, I left for a reason. I have no intention of going back. Why allow for temptation, letting the easy way govern my destiny?

Going back is futile.

I lack the power to change the situation.

I can only learn from the experience.

"Go right," says my inner voice. *"It is right, after all."*

"Right. So it is," I tell myself.

I look right. The path looks smooth. Right turns are always simple. Most times, success follows those who choose the right path. Occurrences align as intended.

The question. Do I desire effortless success? Where does everything proceed as planned?

Perhaps I need a better challenge.

"Fine," my inner voice cautions. *"Avoid the simple path; embrace the challenge. Go left."*

"Yes," I say. "I agree."

Turning left is always a challenge. This requires time. Takes patience. Trust me, the wait alone can test patience.

Don't believe me?

Try making a left into your favorite store off a busy street. Instead, wait for several green lights before turning left; the preceding drivers lack awareness, thus holding you up further.

Skill, sound judgment, and considerable personal exertion are required.

"Your only other option is forward. Straight ahead," my inner voice commands.

This has its merits. I'm leaving the past, sitting here in the present and looking toward the future.

I want to continue the journey. Progress to something better. Move forward; create any label you choose. Risk and uncertainty exist. This might be straightforward. May prove challenging. When you move forward, an enormous factor to deal with is… *the unknown.*

2

So here I sit at a corner. A corner of indecision.

What to do?

What would you do?

13ᵀᴴ
FLOOR

Yard Sale

1

A mild summer day is present, notwithstanding the mid-August Michigan setting.

The temperature isn't too cool, but neither is the heat overwhelming. Branigan Frost deems it a perfect day for a dog walk.

He is a decent sized man out walking his little dachshund, Berrington Bear. 2B for short. Their unusual pairing causes motorists to do double takes. Branigan cares not.

A block away from home, Branigan passes a sign posted on the corner. It reads…

YARD SALE

Nothing out of the ordinary about it. Except for two minor details. First, the sign omits the sale address; second, the sign is pointing into Rosewood Cemetery.

Branigan stops to do a double take. He surveys the area around him and concludes that it shouldn't point ahead of him; there are no homes in that direction. It shouldn't point left either for the same reason. He sees nothing behind; thus, Branigan deduces the sale is down the street to the right.

No one would hold a yard sale in a cemetery. He helpfully redirects the sign, then takes 2B back around the block and home.

2

The next day, Branigan is driving home from work. He passes the corner with the yard sale sign and sees that it's pointing back into the cemetery.

He pulls over and gets out of the car to investigate. Sure enough, someone has moved the sign back into its original position. Based on the evidence, someone has completed the task recently.

A sick joke, he muses as he repositions the sign. Satisfied, he returns to his car to head for home.

Skeletal hands protrude from the earth when Branigan is out of sight. They grab the sign, reversing its direction to point toward Rosewood Cemetery.

3

That evening, unable to sleep, Branigan goes out for a midnight stroll to help clear his mind. His thought process is that the fresh air will do him good.

He walks his regular path, going past the cemetery where he sees someone has again altered the yard sale sign's direction to face the cemetery. Branigan leans down and inspects the surrounding dirt. It has been freshly dug up. Someone has moved the sign recently.

Branigan stands there thinking of a logical explanation for why someone would continue to point a sign for a yard sale into Rosewood Cemetery.

While he stands there, a strange light illuminates the ground behind him. It's not a natural light, more spectral, glowing blueish white.

Branigan turns and gazes into the cemetery itself. What he sees defies comprehension at first glance.

4

Branigan heads down the hill to investigate and enters the cemetery.

As he proceeds along the main path, he goes unnoticed by the dead who have turned the cemetery into an open market. Their caskets serve as tables even though their graves below are undisturbed. Each interred individual offers what they took with them in death.

The cemetery is old. Interments date back over a century. A business executive from the 1940s with a gold pocket watch and a pair of fancy cuff links. Nearby: a 1980s woman, adorned with flashy jewelry trinkets. A soldier, possibly a Civil War veteran, has belongings dating from the 1800s. It's all here for sale, in a manner of speaking.

Yes, the dead have no money. However, the barter system is in full swing and the dead trade back and forth silently.

The unfolding situation overwhelms Branigan as he wanders around, observing.

He watches the dead wander around each other's graves. Trades sometimes occur; other times, only browsing.

When an individual feels they have what they want, they return to their eternal rest by disappearing into thin air.

There's no recollection they were ever *awake.*

Branigan makes the last turn on the main path when one of the departed individuals glimpses the bracelet he wears.

The apparition motions Branigan to come over.

Out of curiosity, he does.

The apparition doesn't speak, just motions to the bracelet.

Branigan sees this and is willing. "You would like this, yes?" he asks, taking it off.

The apparition nods.

He reaches behind him producing a unique gold necklace. He motions, showing Branigan the necklace, then points to the bracelet.

"You want me to trade my bracelet for your necklace?" asks Branigan.

The apparition nods his agreement.

"Done," says Branigan.

They make the exchange.

The apparition, pleased with the trade, bows to Branigan before disappearing in a bright flash. The flash is so bright; it causes Branigan to stumble and fall back. Hitting his head on a gravestone, he blacks out.

5

The alarm clock sounds the next morning, rousing Branigan from a deep slumber. He's groggy and has a splitting headache.

"What a dream," he says to 2B, who lies there on the bed unphased.

He gets up and heads to the bathroom, rubbing the back of his head. A slight bump is present. Branigan has a hazy memory of hitting his head, believing it to be a dream.

Branigan gets the shower going, then turns on the bathroom light. As he looks into the mirror, he realizes it isn't a dream. It happened. For around his neck is the gold necklace he traded for last night. Branigan recounts the incident but finds it hard to accept.

That's until the steam from the shower fogs the mirror, revealing a simple message scrawled onto it.

Thank You

12TH
FLOOR

Arrogance Meets Its Match

1

Gary races down the highway in his pristine arrest-me-red Ford Mustang GT convertible like a bat out of hell, weaving in and out of cars that are moving way too slowly to suit his fancy. To call him careless is an understatement; he's downright *reckless*. And the scary part? He knows it and doesn't care.

Gary cuts across three lanes of traffic, veering off onto his exit at a breakneck speed, not even thinking of slowing down as he merges into the oncoming traffic. He relishes in breaking all speed limits as he goes about a block before whipping into the parking lot of The Shoe Box, nearly clipping a car that is attempting to pull out. In anger, he lays on his horn, flipping off the driver as he burns rubber like a banshee towards *his* parking spot.

Within seconds, he arrives, only to find that someone else has already parked there. "Son of a bitch!" he yells as he slams on the brakes, bringing the car to an abrupt halt. "Who in the hell has the audacity to park in my spot? Don't they know who I am?!"

Gary looks around to see if he can find a suitable alternative. Spotting it, he peels out and skids into it. He secures two spots to deter parking on either side. God help them if they did or even thought about it.

Gary exits the vehicle. He walks around the car and gives it a good once over. Noticing some dust on the passenger side rear fender, he pops the trunk and reaches into a small utility box that lies just inside. Gary goes to work, pulling out a small spray bottle and a chamois cloth, to clean the spot until it shines and sparkles in the sunlight. Satisfied with his efforts, he replaces the bottle and cloth in the utility box, shuts the trunk, and retrieves his suit jacket from the backseat. He throws it over his shoulder with a smug confidence; he shuts the car door, locks the car, and struts across the parking lot.

Gary is a pretty boy, a metrosexual in today's terms. Impeccably groomed with his custom made, tailored suit, he understands he's all that and then some. He knows all the Shoe Box employees envy him and wonder how he can afford such things on the pathetic salary he gets. Gary doesn't give a rat's ass. He knows his shit doesn't stink, and he's proud of it.

As he approaches the store's entrance, Gary puts on his suit jacket and pauses for a moment to primp in the store's front window. Gary puts his arrogant expression on as he walks into the store.

At the register area, a blonde-haired bombshell, named Maria, strains herself to stop filing her nails so she can turn and greet him as the doorbell goes off. "Welcome to the Shoe…" she says, stopping in mid-sentence. She sees its Gary and finishes her greeting saying, "Oh, it's you."

"Yes, it's me baby!" he tells her, "and because it's me, all is right with the world."

Maria rolls her eyes and asks him in a disgusted tone, "How many times, Gary, have I told you…DON'T. CALL. ME. BABY!"

"Let's see, baby, more than once I think," is his response. "But I have a question for you, sweetie."

Maria takes a quick step back as she spontaneously replies, "No, I won't go out with you. You are a two-timing piece of shit!"

"Funny." responds Gary, not impressed. "That wasn't the question."

"Really" replies Maria. She waits for his question, but he doesn't reply. "Well, what?" she asks in an angry tone.

Gary leans in close to her and asks, "Do you know whose piece of shit car that is in my spot?"

Maria gazes out the window to see what Gary is referring to. She rolls her eyes and looks up at the ceiling, not giving him an immediate response. This infuriates him.

"Well…" he says, becoming impatient with her.

"Let's see…I expect that's Jack's car," she tells him, swooning. "He's the new loss prevention manager. And I must tell you…he's hot!"

"Not as hot as I am, baby!"

"Gary," she says, motioning him to come closer to her. She leans in and whispers in his ear, "Call me baby one more time, and I'll make you useless to a woman, not that you aren't already."

Gary takes a step back seeing the sinister expression in Maria's eyes and can only respond by saying "Okay." Composing himself, he politely asks her "And where's Jack so I can have a chat with the boy on proper parking procedures around here?"

Maria takes her time to answer. "I guess…he's in the stockroom with Larry and Jeff," she tells him. "The truck is on its way and they're getting ready for it."

"Well, Jack is going to receive a piece of my mind before he receives that truck!" he tells her before storming off towards the stockroom.

"Whatever, shit-for-brains!" she mutters once he is out of earshot. She leans back against the counter and returns to filing her nails.

2

Unaware of Gary's arrival, Jack takes out the trash and what's left of the previous week's cardboard; meanwhile, Larry and Jeff stack the store's transfers outside the door and finish readying the stockroom for the truck. The three guys are all dressed in jeans and casual polo shirts. It's the one day, for at least Larry and Jeff, when they can dress comfortably, unlike the rest of the week when they are required to adhere to the dress code: shirt and tie, dress slacks, and fancy shoes. Jack can dress however he wants, so he can blend in with customers and not stick out as loss prevention.

Suddenly, the stockroom doors burst open. They slam against the side walls as Gary walks through. He stands there with his hands on his hips as they swing back, closing behind him.

"Well, look who's here…it's Gary," quips Larry. "You're right on time. The truck just pulled in. Ready to get those precious hands of yours dirty?"

"I doubt that will happen, Larry."

"Why's that, Jeff?"

"Because he might break a nail and cry!" says Jeff, holding out his hand and acting in a prissy manner; the sight of which sends Larry rolling into laughter.

"You guys are a couple of comedians," responds Gary, not finding their comments and actions amusing in the least. "I won't soil myself. You're here for the dirty work, not me! I'm the manager and I refuse to lower myself to such standards."

"You're an arrogant little ass now, aren't you?" asks a voice from outside.

Gary doesn't recognize the voice. He asks, "Who said that?"

A large but fit man that bears an uncanny resemblance to Steve Perry of the rock band, Journey comes into view. He takes the last drag of his cigarette and tosses it to the side as he walks into the stockroom. "I did."

"And who the hell do you think you are?" asks Gary.

"Jack Schultz, loss prevention manager. You must be Gary. Nice to meet you," he tells him as he extends his hand for Gary to shake.

Gary looks at Jack's grubby hand in disgust and doesn't return the gesture. "Is that your piece of shit car that is parked in my spot?" asks Gary.

"Watch out! Here it comes… it's the speech!" declares Larry.

With a disdainful glance, Gary stares at Larry and tells him in a stern voice, "If you value your job, you would do well to shut up! I wasn't talking to you. I believe I was talking to Jack."

"Forgive me for speaking out of turn, your hind-ass!" replies Larry. He turns to finish muttering "What an asshole!" as he does.

Gary refocuses his attention towards Jack and says, "Well… I asked you a question and I expect an answer."

Jack strokes his chin for a moment. He responds, "Yes, it's my car. But it's not a piece of shit, it's a classic. And as far as where I'm parked, I don't recall seeing any sign around that states that this spot belongs to Gary."

"Well, that is my spot. Keep this in mind for future reference. You're to park elsewhere. Are we clear?"

"We're clear. Whenever I work, parking is available there. Thanks, Gary! You the man!" Jack tells him in a very cocky manner.

"That's not what I just said, smart ass. Didn't you just hear what I said?"

"Excuse me?" says Jack as he gets up in Gary's face. "I hear what you're saying. I'm just not listening. And for the record, it's mister smart ass. Small m, get it right next time."

"You've got some nerve getting in my face, Jack! What's your last name again?"

"Schultz." Replies Jack.

"Schultz? What kind of name is Schultz, anyway?" Gary asks in a derogatory manner.

"It is a solid German name."

"What a coincidence. My last name is Hirsch. It's a solid Jewish name," Gary responds proudly and puffs up his chest as he gloats.

Tired of Gary's nonsense, Jack pats him hard on the shoulder telling him, "Well hell, son, maybe my grandfather burned your grandfather during the war!"

Larry and Jeff stand there dumbfounded by what Jack has just said. They can't believe he went there. They restrain their laughter and comments while observing Gary, who's always sharp-witted, struggling to respond. He just stands there, unable to speak as he looks at Jack, who just insulted him. Tears fill his eyes as he storms out of the stockroom in silence. Jack got the best of him, and he knows it.

Jack cracks a shit-eating grin and turns around to see Larry and Jeff standing there about to crack up, still shaking their heads in disbelief that he said what he said. Without missing a beat, Jack pretends to look innocent and asks, "Was it something I said?"

11TH
FLOOR

Anatomy Challenge

1

Mr. Avery, City High's anatomy and physiology teacher, walks into his third hour class.

His students, jostling about as they usually do because the bell to start class has yet to ring.

As he walks into the room, he immediately notices his skeleton of "Fritz" the cat, sitting atop his filing cabinet, was "dressed up" in a manner of speaking. It looks like some bad practical effect right out of a B-rated 80s horror film.

Someone, he has a good idea who, placed a pair of bugged out eyeballs into the skull, inserted a severed tongue into the cat's jaw, and then covered the skull with a furry scalp.

As the bell rings, the class settles down. Mr. Avery can't help but look at the *doctored* skeleton of the cat and chuckle.

"Alright," he asks, "Who's the sick bastard that did this?" pointing at the cat's skeleton while scanning the front row of tables for the would-be culprit. All of whom sit trying to look innocent.

After a few moments of uncomfortable silence, his student, Max Hudson, rolls his eyes and, not being to help himself, grins.

Mr. Avery sees this, confirming his assumption of who dressed up Fritz.

"Mr. Hudson. You have a sick sense of humor. You realize that don't you?"

The class bursts into laughter as Max answers, "Yes, I do, sir. However, you must admit the poor thing was looking somewhat… peaked, dead really. He needed to be livened up a bit."

"Mission accomplished, Mr. Hudson. I hope for your sake your knowledge is as sharp as your wit," says Mr. Avery.

"I guarantee you it is, Mr. Avery," responds Max.

"That's good, because I want to inform you all that your mid-term exam is this Friday."

The class groans in unison. Mr. Avery always had to be a buzz kill.

He informs the class, "We will work on dissections today, then review tomorrow, exam on Friday, taking most of the hour."

"I doubt that," says Max. "Can I be exempt?"

"And why is it you believe you should be exempt, Mr. Hudson?" asks Mr. Avery.

"He's the resident know-it-all of third hour, Mr. Avery," says Martha Rossi from the back of the class.

Max looks at Mr. Avery and states, "She's not wrong. I love this subject, and I *am* the best in this class. This mid-term test of yours should be rather easy."

"Little arrogant of you, don't you think, Mr. Hudson?"

"No, sir. Not at all. Just stating a fact."

"I see," says Mr. Avery as he stands there to contemplating the situation. Then it comes to him, "Well, Mr. Hudson, how about a little challenge? Are you up for one?"

"I love an enjoyable challenge, sir. Bring it."

"Here's the skinny," says Mr. Avery. "You will take the mid-term exam. Get a superstar grade and I will give you an automatic *A* on the final exam. I'll excuse you from the final, but attendance is required. Afterwards, you are free to leave. And since you are the resident wiseacre of third hour, as Ms. Rossi pointed out, what will you accomplish in the mid-term?"

"How many minutes should the test take?" asks Max.

"If you know your stuff, as you say you do, have paid attention in class to my lectures, and reviewed the notes and texts, about 45 minutes," says Mr. Avery.

"How many questions?"

"One hundred."

"And the type of questions?"

"Does it matter?"

"Not really. Only for the time factor."

"I see," says Mr. Avery. He tells Max, "There will be matching, multiple choice, and true/false."

"How many am I allowed to miss?" asks Max.

"Well," says Mr. Avery, "If you're as good as you say you are, you shouldn't miss any of them. I'm a good sport. You may miss two."

"And when I am done, I may leave?"

"Yes, Mr. Hudson, you may after attendance."

"So, let me make sure I'm clear on the parameters of the test," says Max. "You are giving us a one hundred question test. This test will have a mix of questions that are matching, multiple choice, and true/false. Being prepared allows one to finish the test within 45 minutes. If I exceed my goals, I'll receive an automatic A on the final exam and won't have to come to class that day, except for attendance. This is the gauntlet you are handing to me?"

"You are correct, Mr. Hudson, on all counts," confirms Mr. Avery.

"Mr. Avery," says Max, "I accept your gauntlet, and I expand the challenge. I will come in and whip through your exam. My conditions are: I won't miss more than one, though perfection will be the goal. I'll also have it done in only fifteen minutes. Piece of cake, sir."

The class falls silent at the terms that Max has laid out for Mr. Avery. So quiet one could hear a pin drop. (No pun intended here.)

Mr. Avery himself stands in disbelief at this brash statement. After a moment, he answers, "Very well, Mr. Hudson. Challenge accepted. I cannot wait to see this."

Max holds out his hand. Mr. Avery accepts, and they shake in agreement.

As Max lets go, Mr. Avery tightens his grip and tells him, "Mr. Hudson, fail and the crow of my choosing will be on the menu."

Max smiles. "I would expect no less, sir."

"Alright, everyone," says Mr. Avery. "Let's get down to business. Get out your specimens and we will pick up where we left off yesterday. Mr. Hudson."

"Yes, sir," answers Max.

"See that you take care of your cat's parts on Fritz up there before leaving today."

"Not a problem, Mr. Avery."

The class gets up from their seats and does as Mr. Avery has instructed.

One of Max's dissection partners comes up to him, "Dude, you are freaking insane. I hope for your sake you know what the hell you are doing."

"Have faith, my friend," says Max as he removes the parts of his cat from Fritz's skeleton.

2

Test Day: Friday—2 Days Later

Mr. Avery walks into his third hour class. He briefly stops to ensure Fritz is un*altered*. He notices that the class today seems focused on the upcoming mid-term exam, as they are quieter than normal.

The starting bell rings, and Mr. Avery reaches into his briefcase to retrieve the test packets. "Here is your mid-term exam," he tells the class as he passes them out, placing them face down in front of each student. He saves Max's for last.

"You will have the entire hour to complete the exam. Also, to keep all of you honest, each test differs from that of your neighbor's."

A few groans arise from the class in response to the statement.

Mr. Avery looks at his pocket watch. As the exam is about to begin, he announces to the class, "Mr. Hudson has until 10:25 a.m. to finish. Per our discussion the other day, if he achieves his criteria, I will honor our agreement and wish him… good luck."

The classroom fills with the rustling of test packets being turned over. He tells the class, "You may begin," as his watch hits 10:10 a.m.

Max glances at classroom's clock to get his bearing on the time. Fat chance as Mr. Avery covered it with a sign that reads…

Time Will Pass… Will you?

No matter.

He whips through the questions with ease. The packet that he has starts with matching diagrams of the systems, placing the corresponding letter of the organ in the proper spot. Done.

True/false next up on the docket, around twenty questions. Done.

Multiple choice rounds out the exam. Around twenty-five questions, and soon this section falls.

Max spends a minute to peruse his answers, then stands up to a universal classroom gasp as he hands his exam to Mr. Avery, the time being 10:17 a.m.

"Will that be all, Mr. Avery?" asks Max.

"You're so sure of yourself, Mr. Hudson?" queries Mr. Avery.

"Yes, sir. Done in half the time, I agreed to, and the test is perfect."

"We shall see, Mr. Hudson."

Mr. Avery looks at Max's test booklet number and pulls out the corresponding answer key. He meticulously goes through page-by-page, checking Max's responses to that of the answer key. As he finishes the last page, he looks up at Max in utter shock. The student's self-assessment is accurate.

"Class, if I may interrupt. I'd like to announce that your classmate, Mr. Max Hudson, has successfully accomplished his challenge that he laid down to me. His terms were only one wrong in fifteen minutes. He achieved a perfect score in half the time, in under ten minutes. As per our agreement, Max will receive an automatic A on the final exam. He can also skip class on that day. I'll even fudge the attendance, as I am impressed."

"May I leave, sir?" asks Max.

"Get the hell out of here, Mr. Hudson," says Mr. Avery.

Max collects his things and leaves to thunderous applause from his classmates. As he opens the classroom door to leave, Mr. Avery says to him, "Mr. Hudson. Job well done. Have a good weekend."

Max smiles.

"Thank you, sir," he responds as he exits, closing the door behind him.

10TH
FLOOR

A "*Lion King*" Tale

Seems like yesterday I was calling you *Mogwai*, because in the first photo taken of you, you looked like Gizmo from *Gremlins*. I don't call you *Mogwai* any longer, though I still refer to you as *Lil One*. You are far from it. You've grown into a beautiful, smart woman.

Over the years, you've matured, graduated high school, graduated college, forged out a career, and married your soul mate all within the blink of an eye. You've known triumph, dealt with loss, and in both, have done so with both grace and strength. Now, you are adding a new title to your repertoire… Mother. I know you will be one of the best around.

Motherhood comes with many challenges. Trust me, I put your grandmother through many in my lifetime. One of those challenges is to get your son/daughter to go to sleep. As I recall, it was a challenge most nights with you, back when you were knee high to a grasshopper.

No matter the challenge, one thing did the trick every single time… listening to the soundtrack to your favorite film, *The Lion King*. Didn't matter which bed you got tucked into yours; grandma's; or mine; put that soundtrack on, and within minutes, you were out. Some nights were quicker than others. What is it about that soundtrack? No clue, but it always did the trick though. Most likely because it's uplifting, very positive, and has that relaxing feel in the music. It also works to write to, as I am listening to it as I write you this brief story/note.

I'm sure that you will receive many splendid gifts for your *Lil One*. My gift is more sentimental. I always intended to pass this to you. Didn't see how… until you announced you were expecting. So, enclosed with this brief story/note is my original CD of the soundtrack to *The Lion King*, the same one I played night after night to get you to fall asleep. I pass it on to you for your *Lil One*, hoping on nights that you are having a hard time getting them down to sleep, it will help calm them down, relax them and put them to sleep much like it did you so many years ago.

CONGRATULATIONS!

Uncle Wolverton

Love,
Your Uncle Wolverton

9TH
FLOOR

The Imagination Of A 5-Year-Old

1

My five-year-old grandson walks into the bathroom as I am trimming my beard and mustache.

"What are you doing, Opa?" he asks.

"I'm trimming up my mustache and beard," I answer.

"Why?"

Typical five-year-old. Needs that extra explanation to the simplest of answers. He so loves making mountains out of molehills. So, I explain, "Because, Nana said Opa is looking scruffy and I'm eating my mustache," showing him how long it is and that I can chew on it.

He giggles. "I want to help," he says.

"Unfortunately, you can't help with this, buddy."

"Why not? I *am* a barber," he informs me.

"You are," I say, astonished. "Aren't you a little young to be a barber?"

"Nope!" he confidently exclaims.

He can do anything he sets his mind to.

As I finish up, my grandson watches and makes silly statements. He also assists me with brushing the loose whiskers off my arms, neck, and chest.

As I put everything away and clean up, my grandson opens a drawer, pulling out the hairbrush he uses.

"These are my clippers," he states. "I am the barber. You came to have a haircut."

"Okay," I say, playing along. "But Opa needs to finish up something in his office. Can you cut my hair in there?"

"YES!" he yells, grabbing his stool so he can reach my head as we walk into my office.

2

I sit down at my desk as he positions his stool. He thus *pretends* to cut my hair.

"So. Tell me about your day," he says, making conversation as your everyday barber would do.

"Oh, it was very long. Very boring and not much else to say about it," I say as I continue to update my bank accounts and check my email.

"You know, Opa, this would be much easier if I sat behind you."

"No, you don't need to sit behind me."

"Yes, I do. Please, Opa."

"Okay," I tell him, giving in. Sometimes it is the better part of valor to give in.

My grandson climbs into my chair behind me. He continues to make cutting sounds until I hear him say, "Oops!" and then giggles like a hyena.

"Oops?! What do you mean, oops? Oops isn't good. What… did you… do?"

"I made you bald, Opa!"

"Wait! You gave you Opa a Captain Picard haircut?"

"Yup!" he says proudly. "Don't worry, Opa. I can fix it."

"Okay, I won't worry," I tell him. "You fix it."

"K," he says as he climbs up and sits on my shoulders.

"Excuse me," I say. "What are you doing?"

He gives me the obvious answer. "I'm sitting on your shoulders."

"Why?" I ask.

"To cut your hair," he answers.

"But you just said you made Opa bald. How can you cut my hair if you did that? And I don't think barbers sit on shoulders."

"I do," he says.

"You are a barber, right?" I ask.

"Yes. Who cuts hair," he answers.

"While sitting on shoulders?"

"Yes."

"I understand," I tell him.

My grandson continues his *work* and then makes a spraying sound.

"What are you doing now?" I ask.

"Painting your hair white," he responds.

"And why are you doing this?"

"So you can't see that you are bald. I told you I am a barber who cuts hair."

I repeat, like this is some Abbot and Costello routine, "You are a barber who cuts hair while sitting on shoulders. And you make people bald."

"Yes, and I paint their hair white so they can't see it," he chimes in and adds, "Let's go tell, Nana."

"Okay," I tell him as I stand up from my chair. My grandson is still atop my shoulders as we walk into the living room.

"What is this?" asks Nana.

"Tell her, Opa," my grandson insists.

"This is our grandson. He would like me to tell you he is a barber, who cuts hair while sitting on shoulders. He makes people bald, then paints their hair white, so they can't see that they are bald."

"I understand," says Nana as she shakes her head and smiles in disbelief.

There you have it, my friends. The imagination of a five-year-old.

8TH
FLOOR

The Wahenee Splash

Family pets do some funny, and sometimes weird, things to one another. Describing what happened to one would be easy, but perhaps not as amusing as watching it happen.

However, consider visualizing such an incident as a play-by-play call in a sporting event. Here's the transcript of the incident.

BEGIN TRANSCRIPT.

Ken Englehart: Welcome everyone to MONDAY. NIGHT. PAW! I'm Ken Englehart alongside my broadcast partner Oswald "The Wizard" Henkle. Tonight, we are coming to you live from The Kitchen, here on the beautiful northeast side of Grand Rapids, Michigan.

Oswald Henkle: Kenny, take a glance at this arena. A retro 1950s kitchen complete with a ceramic tile backsplash. Not sure what moron picked this putrid teal color, but it seems to work. Solid oak cabinets made with old German craftsmanship; granite countertops and modern stainless-steel appliances finish this fashion. It's a shame; it could become a real mess in here tonight!

Ken Englehart: Messy is one way to put it with the potential mismatch we have here this evening.

Oswald Henkle: Potential mismatch?! What the hell are you smoking, Kenny?! This matchup is a mismatch of epic proportions, and I am talking, *epic!* If I were the challenger, I'd walk away. There's no shame in it and no one would blame her.

Ken Englehart: Well, Oz, it doesn't appear our challenger tonight is going to walk away as she makes her way to the ring. Let's go down to our ring announcer, Allen Finkbeiner.

Allen Finkbeiner: The following matchup, scheduled for one fall, and it is for the House Pet Championship! In the ring is the challenger. She's "The Pom Chi Cutie", who hails from Hale, Michigan. Weighing in at five pounds… TESS-A-ROOO!

Oswald Henkle: Look at Tess-A-Roo, Kenny. Prancing around The Kitchen looking all cute and lovable. Makes me sick! It's sad she's oblivious to what awaits her.

Ken Englehart: Well, Oz, regardless, Tess-A-Roo signed up for this match. That Chihuahua spirit in her says she's feisty and won't back down from a challenge.

Oswald Henkle: She may have second thoughts about that as here comes the House Pet Champion.

Ken Englehart: Let's go back down to our ring announcer.

Allen Finkbeiner: Approaching the ring, her opponent and reigning House Pet Champion of the World, "The Tortoise Shell Tabby", hailing from Stanwood, Michigan, weighing in at twenty-three pounds, Momma Wahenee (pronounced Wah-He-Nee) … MIA!

Ken Englehart: My God, Oz! Check out the size of Momma Wahenee! She's over four times the size of Tess-A-Roo. The challenger faces a hell of a tough uphill battle.

The starting bell sounds.

Ken Englehart: And with the sounding of the bell, the match is underway. Mia has yet to enter the ring, Oz. What do you make of it?

Oswald Henkle: Its psychological warfare by the champion, Kenny. She's sitting outside the ring, crouching, waiting for the right moment to make her move. Meanwhile, her opponent, Tess-A-Roo, prances around the ring, wanting to play.

Ken Englehart: I don't think Mia is in a playing mood tonight, Oz.

Oswald Henkle: Kenny, when this is all done, Tess-A-Roo will wish Mia wanted to…

Ken Englehart: (Interrupting) Here comes the champion, running full speed into the ring! She looks like she is charging the challenger. Tess-A-Roo barks at Mia but she's not fazed in the least. She leaps into the air.

Oswald Henkle: She's going to the countertop, Kenny, to gain the higher ground!

Ken Englehart: WAIT A MINUTE, OZ! She isn't going to higher ground! Mia is using the countertop as a springboard. Now in midair, she flattens herself and comes crashing down on the unsuspecting challenger!

Oswald Henkle: IT'S THE WAHENEE SPLASH! Mia nailed it out of nowhere! Tess-A-Roo is out of there!
Tess-A-Roo's eyes bug out from their sockets, and she yelps as Mia lands on top of her, squashing her hard and pinning her to the floor.

The referee calls for the bell.

The bell rings.

Allen Finkbeiner: Here is your winner, and STILL House Pet Champion, Momma Wahenee…MIA!

Momma Wahenee Mia exits the ring like nothing ever happened. Turning, she watches as her flattened opponent attempts to get up, seeing stars. Satisfaction is her reward this evening, and she relishes it as she struts away.

Ken Englehart: This one was over in a heartbeat, Oz!

Oswald Henkle: It wasn't even a beat, Kenny! This one was over before it started. Great tactics by the champion.

Oswald provides commentary while the replay is being shown.

Oswald Henkle: Momma Wahenee sits outside the ring. Patiently waiting for the perfect opportunity. As it arrives, she charges her opponent but fakes her out at the last second. She leaps to the countertop and uses it to execute a perfect Wahenee Splash, squashing the life out of the challenger. Match over!

Ken Englehart: Tess-A-Roo makes her way out of the ring, still in a daze. An exciting, albeit short, championship match here tonight. We'll take a break with some words from your local pet suppliers. More Monday Night Paw is on the way…NEXT!

CUT FOR COMMERCIAL.

END TRANSCRIPT.

7TH
FLOOR

A Visit From Krampus:
A 6-Year-Old's Revenge

1

Gabriel is in tears as he's forced to watch the other family members open their gifts for Christmas. He cannot partake and nor did he didn't any gifts this year. Santa himself couldn't save this child's Christmas. He can thank his mom and stepfather for that.

They informed him he hadn't been behaving and had made many poor decisions. His consequence for that is no Christmas.

Consequences of his actions?

What six-year-old understands the concept? Okay, he might; I got caught doing something bad. No Nintendo Switch. I told a fib. No watching television. He grasps the core idea and its underlying logic but to cancel his Christmas and force him to bear witness! That's going over the edge.

Mom, however, jumps at everything the child's stepfather says. She is nothing more than the man's puppet. This shit wouldn't have flown when she was a single mom. Now, however, she is nothing more than a sheep and follows without question.

Nana and Opa disapprove of their daughter's latest escapade. They told her so in no uncertain terms. She turned her nose up and asked them just who in the hell did they think they were, inserting themselves in her family's affairs. She'd handle her son's consequences. And if they had an issue with it, they could go pound sand!

That little tirade had consequences for her. Opa told his own daughter to pound sand! He retrieved every gift, including those meant for his other grandson; then firmly explained Christmas's true meaning. He even refused the gifts she had given them.

Gabriel goes into a teary meltdown because of this. He begs and pleads for Nana and Opa not to go. It falls on deaf ears as they slam the door behind them.

As Gabriel watches his grandparents depart, both his mother and his stepfather tell him in unison to take his crying ass to his room. They've reached their limit; settlement will follow.

Gabriel defiantly complies, as it's pointless to argue.

He of all people knows his mother and stepfather are more like overlords than parents, and they favor their child implicitly.

2

As Gabriel sits alone in his room, he wants revenge. He wants mommy and his stepfather to suffer like them make him. Such thoughts aren't healthy for one of his age.

Giving up on Christmas, Gabriel finds a toy to entertain himself.

From a dark corner, a voice speaks. "So, young master," it says in a growly voice. "We've been a tad naughty this year, have we not?"

Gabriel turns around and looks into the corner.

He sees nothing.

"I suppose I have," he says. "But my mommy and step daddy have been worse."

"I see," says the voice. "It still doesn't excuse your actions, young master."

"Where are you?" asks Gabriel.

"I'm right in front of you," says the voice as two yellow demonic eyes appear from nowhere.

Gabriel staggers back as the eyes proceed from the shadow to reveal their full and true form.

A massive figure, dark hair, horns curling from its head, long bony fingers tipped with claws. Its facial features are goat-like. Its beard is dripping with saliva from the long and slinky tongue that flicks from its mouth. Birch sticks fill one hand, a chain with bells in the other.

"Do you know who I am, young master?" asks the creature.

"Yes," replies Gabriel. "Opa has told me stories about you. He warned me that if I didn't shape up, I'd be seeing you… Krampus, instead of Saint Nicholas."

"Your Opa is a wise man, Gabriel. He knows his lore," acknowledges Krampus.

Krampus strokes his chin and tells Gabriel, "I should have come for you sooner as you deserve punishment for being naughty," he adds, "But today is not that day."

"Why?" asks Gabriel.

"Your behavior, Gabriel, has been atrocious this year. Though it is not all your fault. Most of it reflects your mother and stepfather's actions toward you. This is inexcusable and they deserve to be punished for it. Wouldn't you agree?"

"Yes," answers Gabriel.

"So be it," states Krampus. "I will do my job, young master. However, I expect you to be on your best behavior from now till next St. Nicholas Day. I'll be back; any deviation from expectations will have serious consequences. Do you understand what I am saying?"

"Yes, sir," answers Gabriel.

"Good," says Krampus as he swats Gabriel with the birch sticks.

Gabriel doesn't cry, but his reaction is that of confusion.

Krampus sees this and tells him, "That is for your actions, young master, for this year, and a subtle reminder to behave for next year. Should you misbehave, next year will bring harsher consequences upon my return."

Krampus walks to the door of Gabriel's room.

"You are to stay here until I am gone." Krampus, appearing like a ghost, instructs him, "You'll know when it's time."

3

Gabriel listens as Krampus performs his assigned task.

He hears his mother scream and his stepfather wail as whipping sounds crack throughout the living room.

His baby brother cries out only for a brief second, then silence.

The door to his bedroom opens.

Gabriel hesitates a moment, then heads down the hall from his room.

4

Gabriel walks into the living room, observing the carnage Krampus has left behind.

His stepfather lies in the middle of the room. He's not dead, but is barely alive. His face and arms scratched and bloodied from the birch sticks that Krampus brutally beat him with.

Gabriel's mother, also barely conscience, attempts to rise to get her bearings. She scrambles to reach her infant son, stuffed inside a burlap sack.

Unfastening the sack, she takes out her son. She's relieved to find he only has a few minor scratches on him.

The floor boards of the room creak behind her.

She spins around to see Gabriel standing there smiling with a devilish grin planted on his face, pleased with what he sees.

Confused by his demeanor, his mother asks, "Why?"

Gabriel stands silent. He then answers maturely, "Because, Mother, you, my stepfather, and my brother were disobedient. Considerably disobedience. Krampus came to make it right. I suggest you heed his warning and be thankful he didn't give you worse. Next time, you won't be as lucky."

Gabriel turns and goes back to his room.

He hears his mother scream as she sees Krampus reappear. His beady yellow eyes stare her down as if to say, *I am protecting the boy.*

"This has been but a warning," says Krampus, his voice echoes before disappearing.

That was a warning, she thinks to herself. With dread, she imagines genuine retribution and passes out, thinking she doesn't wish to find out.

6TH
FLOOR

The Demons Always Catch Up

1

Detective Jim Dyer pulls up to the scene at 620 Grove Street in a small neighborhood in the Petoskey area. Grove Street: a faded, old-fashioned neighborhood. The neighborhood fosters a strong sense of community and mutual support. It is the last place Detective Dyer ever thought he would respond to a 10-56 call (suicide).

He maneuvers down the street, dodging the many patrol cars lining the street or parked in the driveways of the houses leading up to the residence in question.

Finally, finding a place to park after multiple attempts, Detective Dyer exits his vehicle.

He makes his way toward the off-white house, that's bathed in a collage of blue and red swirling lights. It reminds him of the old Bomb Pops that his mother used to give him and his friends on a hot summer afternoon to help them cool off.

Detective Dyer stops at the foot of the driveway for an officer to check his credentials. He then moves under the yellow taped-off area and up to the house.

Once inside, a fellow police officer directs him to the incident; a back bedroom just off the kitchen.

As he enters the room, the grisly scene presents itself.

2

It's a scene not for the faint of heart.

What was once a beautiful young lady, mid-thirties at best, lies against the wall with half her head blown off; skull, brain fragments and blood spattered up the wall where she lay. She shot herself with the .44 magnum that she was holding in her lifeless hand.

She's dressed in a simple pair of blue jeans, a t-shirt, and a pair of old Ked slip-on sneakers. Despite the chaos she left, her room was in order. Nothing appears out of place or disturbed.

Detective Dyer gives the room a final once over before turning his attention to the coroner, who, with another crime scene investigator (CSI), is processing the scene.

"So, Borris, what do you have for me this evening?" asks Detective Dyer.

"Well, Jimmy, what I have for you appears to be your garden variety classic suicide. Victim's name is Tiffany Hart. From what I can tell, the young lady put the barrel of the gun underneath her chin, and bang," motioning with his arms to show the way everything spattered. "She slumped over afterwards but kept a firm grip on the gun. We'll have to pry it out of her hand."

".44 Magnum?" questions Detective Dyer.

"Yup. Guess she believed in the *Dirty Harry* philosophy with this gun."

"Indeed," responds Detective Dyer. "Always a sad sight to see. Any clues showing this wasn't a suicide?"

"Not that I can see. No visible signs of a struggle. Room was tidy when her friend found her. No forced entry; a friend discovered the unlocked front door."

"Well, she lives in a pleasant neighborhood. So, not much of a surprise. However, she desired discovery."

Detective Dyer ponders the remark and then looks around. Then it hits him. "Did anyone find a note?" he asks.

"No, sir," responds the CSI.

"Isn't there always a note?" asks Borris.

"Usually," answers Detective Dyer, "But it appears not this time. Makes you wonder what she was thinking and what drove her to do this…"

3

Earlier that evening:

Twilight settles in on the ever-quiet neighborhood of Grove Street.

It grew darker today, which is unusual for this time of year. Perhaps it is the thick fog that appears out of nowhere and spreads through the neighborhood, engulfing everything in its path.

As the fog engulfs another house on the street, Tiffany Hart comes dashing out of the fog, running as if her life depends on it.

She gets a few feet in front of the fog when she trips, sliding through the grass to a stop. Gathering her senses, she gazes at the approaching fog bank. In it, she swears she sees multiple sets of eyes. Their stares piercing through her.

Tiffany also hears voices, or what sounds like voices, calling out to her. They're mumbling gibberish and make little to no sense. Except for the lead set. What it says is unmistakable.

"Where do you think you can run to, Tiffany?" it asks. *"You've made your decisions. You can't outrun us."*

"WRONG!" screams Tiffany.

She gets up and brushes herself off. Her house is nearby.

Though it is close, it appears to get farther and farther away as the fog surrounds her, leaving only a single shot to it.

With a last-ditch effort, Tiffany takes off in a dead sprint seconds before a phantom hand can grab hold of her.

"There is no escaping, Tiffany. Your time is up. We will have you this evening. This is a forgone conclusion."

Tiffany only glances back once, keeping focused giving on her house. *I'll be secure once I'm inside.* She is certain of it.

As fast as she's running, the fog (and whatever is in it) is keeping pace.

Tiffany makes it to the door. She reaches into her pants pocket, pulls out her keys, and fumbles for the key for the lock. Shaking, she pauses, then unlocks and opens the door.

She makes it inside mere seconds before the fog engulfs her home.

Tiffany locks the door behind her. She runs into the kitchen, frantically looking for something to defend herself with. She then remembers the gun that is stored in her bedroom.

A clicking sound comes from behind her.

She spins around and watches as the front door flies open. The fog creeps its way into the house like a soapy foam coming out of an overflowing washing machine. It fills the house in a slow and methodical manner.

Tiffany rushes into the bedroom. With no time to waste, she retrieves the gun from its locked box just inside the closet. It is her good fortune that she forgot to lock it. She pulls the gun out, loads it with a single shot and crouches up against the wall, tears streaming down her face.

"Why has it come to this?" asks Tiffany, sobbing.

"Because it has," says the voice. *"You made your choices. Poor choices. Ignored the consequences. Now...we are here."*

Tiffany looks at the bedroom doorway to see two sinister, yellowish red eyes appear. The thing's form is not quite human, more like Frankenstein. It slowly advances toward her.

"One shot and you're toast, motherfucker!" warns Tiffany.

"Foolish girl. Don't you realize? You've lost. How, when, all decided," the phantom declares.

"BULLSHIT!" yells Tiffany.

"Perhaps. But everything is in place. You've created your demons. We are here. No matter how hard you try, it... is... too... late. You cannot outrun us any longer."

"I beg to differ," says Tiffany.

With no hesitation, she puts the barrel of the gun underneath her chin and pulls the trigger.

5TH
FLOOR

A Tale Of St. Nicholas

Adapted From The Screenplay Nicholas Of Myra—The Untold Origin Of An Age-Old Legend By Gerald Hartke

1

New York City, December 5, 1822

Dusk falls upon the unique snow-covered cityscape that is New York City. Many of the city's streets remain untouched, covered by a fluffy white blanket of fresh snow. One street is not as fortunate as a sleigh runner slices across the surface, leaving snowflakes fluttering in its wake.

Dr. Clement Moore, a well-dressed middle-aged Englishman, guides his horse-drawn sleigh through the city. He knows his destination as he turns down an empty street. He brings the horse and sleigh to a swift stop in front of the St. Nicholas Orphanage.

Securing the reins, Dr. Moore departs the sleigh and makes his way up a small flight of steps to the orphanage's front door. He composes himself, then knocks on the door.

A young woman answers the door, "Good evening," she says.

"Good evening," responds Dr. Moore. "My name is Doctor Clement Moore. I'm here to see Mr. Livingston."

"A pleasure, sir. Won't you please come in," motioning him inside.

Dr. Moore enters as the woman shuts the door behind him.

"Mr. Livingston is expecting you," she says to him. "May I take your coat and hat?"

"Yes, thank you," answers Moore as he takes off his hat and coat and hands them both to her.

The voices of children from a room just off the foyer drew Dr. Moore's attention. Intrigued, he walks to the doorway to investigate.

2

Dr. Moore peers into what appears to be a library. He sees children sitting near a man with a brown beard, roughly his age. Moore deduces this is Andrew Livingston, the principal of the orphanage.

Moore peers around the room that is decorated with festive candles and lush evergreen garlands.

Along the windowsill, neatly arranged side-by-side, are children's shoes, one for each child.

Andrew Livingston displays his delightful grin to the children. As he speaks, he glimpses Dr. Moore standing in the foyer.

Dr. Moore smiles and nods to Livingston to convey he need not get up.

Livingston returns the gesture and turns his attention back to the children.

Dr. Moore stands and listens as Livingston speaks to the children with his subtle Dutch accent. "Tomorrow is not just a day for *feasting*, children. It's a day of *celebration*…in remembrance of the good saint."

"If the Feast Day is celebrated to remember him, does that mean Saint Nicholas no longer lives?" asks one young boy.

Livingston hesitates as he looks over at Dr. Moore. Moore smiles and glances at Livingston, anticipating his response.

"Oh, dear boy," says Livingston, "He still exists! He exists now in an endless winter."

Giving a nod to the children, he explains, "And whenever a new winter approaches, it *beckons* his return…when he shall bring joy to all good children who await him. For centuries, he has visited on the fifth of December, the *eve* of his Feast Day!"

Livingston takes a slight pause and announces joyfully in broken Dutch, "Feest dit u Sinterklaas!"

The children look at one another with awe-inspired glances.

Dr. Moore, seeing their reactions and continues to listen with great interest as another young boy asks, "If he really does exist…why does everyone not believe in him?"

Livingston looks upon the children's faces, each patiently awaiting his response in silence.

"Everyone is not raised with the same beliefs," he tells them.

"The older boys…raised here in the orphanage…why do they not believe?" asks the boy.

Livingston appears flustered by the question. He explains, "There are some…who know not what it means to believe in something…or someone. To believe in him, you need not believe in myths or magic. You need only believe in devotion, generosity, and all the things he stands for. To believe in him means you open your heart to his spirit, at least one day a year, welcoming the joy that he brings."

Smiling, he pauses a moment and concludes, "And more importantly, giving joy to others in the spirit of his name."

His answer brings to their young minds both an understanding and content. They sit in wonder of Livingston's story for a few minutes before he sends them off to bed.

4TH
FLOOR

May The 4ᵗʰ Be With You

1

This story is appropriate for the day, since it's May 4, 2023. Yes, it's *Star Wars Day*! MAY THE 4ᵗʰ BE WITH YOU!

Did you know the Conservative Party of England originated the phrase May The 4th Be With You in 1979? The party did so to wish Margaret Thatcher well after being elected Prime Minister of England. She took her oath of office on May 4, 1979.

Star Wars Day was first celebrated in Toronto, Canada, in 2011. It has been a huge celebration since *Disney* purchased *Lucasfilm* in 2012.

Star Wars Day wouldn't exist if a little film named *Star Wars* hadn't taken the world by storm back on May 25, 1977.

Star Wars' release is a memory that still resonates with me to this day…

2

Petoskey, Michigan—May/June 1977

I was five years old, soon to be six, when I first learned about a movie called *Star Wars*. I remember seeing it advertised all over television while I watched my afternoon cartoons. The ads also ran during evening shows like *The Wonderful World Of Disney* and the *Star Trek* reruns I watched with my dad on Saturday afternoons.

I'm sure that I pestered my parents to go see it. They released the film on May 25, 1977. Since Petoskey was a small town, most films didn't come to our local theatre until a week or two after their national release. That's how it worked back then.

My dad decided it would be best if we went to a show during the week, figuring it would be less crowded than going on the weekend. Boy, was he wrong!

The Wednesday night after *Star Wars* debuted in Petoskey, Dad took me to see it. We drove from our house on Grove Street, downtown to the movie theatre which, if my memory serves, stood at the bottom of the street on East Mitchell.

I don't think parking was difficult. Yes, I question this as that was forty-six years ago! Remember, I was five, for God's sake. I'm sure it is quite different today from back then. But I digress. We parked and walked to over to the theatre.

Our local theatre was a large building. Out front hung an old-fashioned marquee sign that someone had to climb a ladder each week to change out the title of the current film.

The box office sat in the center of two sets of double doors: one for entering, the other for exiting. Posters and movie stills decorated the walls to each side of the box office. Current attractions were on the side you entered, coming attractions were on the side you exited.

As my dad and I walked up, we could see a massive line. And I mean massive from the perspective of a five-year-old. The line stretched from the box office, down the theatre's front, around the block, and ended at the building's end.

"Look at all these people! We're never going to get in," I told my dad in a panic.

My dad, much calmer, reassured me we would as we got in line.

To my surprise, the line started moving, and it really didn't take that long to reach the box office. My dad and I were lucky we got there when we did. The box office closed after selling the last tickets to the people behind us.

3

The smell of freshly popped popcorn hit me as we walked into the lobby. Reds and gold were the lighting theme that gave the lobby an amber glow. They decorated the walls with vintage movie posters from a by-gone era, along with some more recent films that would become classics one day.

The concession stand sat along the back wall of the lobby. That is where you found the good stuff: fresh hot buttered (real) popcorn, box candies, and pop (soda for those of you who are non-Michiganders). The bathrooms were to the left; to the right, the auditorium doors. The doors had a unique arched design, not square like you would usually expect.

After getting our goodies, my dad and I headed to the auditorium doors. We handed our tickets to the theatre attendant, who dressed like someone from a marching band. He wore a red uniform trimmed with multiple gold buttons. He also wore a small cap held by a chinstrap. Reminded me of a dancing monkey's suit. You know, the ones who dance around with an organ grinder.

"Welcome," he said as he took our tickets. "I suggest you go up to the balcony for your seats," he told us with an accent I hadn't heard before. "The view will be amazing for the young lad."

Yes, you heard that right…a balcony! Something you no longer see in movie theatres today.

My dad thanked him and, taking his advice, we climbed the stairs and walked out to find no seats available. My dad observed the auditorium below, finding it was much the same.

"I think they oversold the theatre tonight," commented my dad.

He did spot one seat in the balcony's front row. I remember telling him I would sit on the step next to the seat as the view of the screen from that spot was dead centered and perfect.

Dad didn't argue. He knew I was excited to watch the movie. When the usher came to check for any empty seats, he also said nothing. He too was aware the theatre was beyond capacity.

The lights dimmed and after a couple of previews for coming attractions, the *20th Century Fox* logo came on the screen with its signature music. The screen faded to black and those famous words in light blue came on screen…

A long time ago, in a galaxy far, far away…

Everyone in the theatre cheered as the *Star Wars* logo appeared on screen followed by the famous title crawl rolling up the screen.

4

For the next two hours and one minute, I sat on that balcony step, mesmerized by everything I took in…images of iconic entrances (yet to be iconic), desert landscapes, strange creatures, intense space battles, and old-fashioned sword fights with laser swords became etched into my memory.

After the film, I remember being on a high. I was so pumped after seeing the movie. It was all I could talk about. When we got home, I rambled and sputtered on about the film to my mom, who had stayed home that night with my sister. My parents did everything, short of grounding me, to get me to bed. Being a school night, I was up way past my bedtime.

I fell asleep thinking about nothing but *Star Wars*. It's hard to believe that this movie sparked my interest in films, their scores, and filming.

This experience also provided me with a memory of a simpler time. One I can still recall and will never forget as long as I live. It was one of those few perfect days you get in a lifetime.

In closing, I say to you…

MAY THE 4ᵀᴴ BE WITH YOU!
ALWAYS.

3RD
FLOOR

The Master's Hand

Wednesday.

I call them Writing Wednesdays, and that's how they have become to be known.

I walk into the office. Daylight streams through open window blinds, illuminating my space. I turn on my desk lamp to add to it. One needs good lighting to write.

I reposition my comfortable office chair at the desk, sit, and put my coffee on the fleur-de-lis coaster in the upper right corner of my desk.

While my Mac Book powers up, I wait. Seconds later, with my password entered, it's time to open the music app and choose the music of the day.

What will inspire me today? Perhaps a movie score or a little Garth Brooks? Maybe a little rock & roll with some Pat Benatar or KISS? Christmas music?

Yes, Christmas music indeed!

Although out of season, this type of music inspires me. I possess a superb classic Christmas playlist. The good stuff from the 1940s, 50s, and 60s. Although my preference is not modern Christmas music, I make exceptions for the groups For King & Country and Trans-Siberian Orchestra because of their exceptional talent with the music of the season.

Headphones are on and adjusted.

I reach for my pad of paper off to my right. Then I pick up the Zebra F-301 0.7 pen my father gave me. It's a unique pen, and it's been used to write every novel I've composed thus far.

I think a moment, click my pen and start the music.

With pen to paper, an unseen force takes over. Sometimes, starts are slow, yet momentum builds relentlessly.

I effortlessly guide my thoughts and words to my hand, flowing them onto the paper with my pen. My current story chapter ignores the passage of time. Coffee and music breaks punctuate my work.

Pages flow. One, two… I lose count until the chapter I am working on is complete. Sometimes the page count is small, three or four. Others are larger, ten, fifteen or more. Any number required to propel the story's progress.

How's this done? Perhaps it's the love of the subject. Or is the music's mood, or my reaction to it, the cause? Perhaps it is the love of my family and friends whom I model my characters after?

Which is it? The answer is vague. It can be anything. Perhaps it's everything combined. I'm certain divine influence explains it all.

How can I say this? Easy. My books seem to have written themselves. The Master's guiding hand empowers and inspires my work. His influence is the origin of my ideas and talent. I am thankful for this.

Amen.

2ND
FLOOR

Till Books Do Us Part

1

A deal with Death always has a catch. Trust me on this, as I have first-hand knowledge.

I was cleaning my office on a sunny Sunday afternoon. I own a modest collection of books. Two hundred twenty-three exactly. At least once a month, I remove the books from the shelves to dust. Before I return the books to their proper place, they also receive a thorough Swiffer dusting. Even though they don't get too dusty, I take good care of them.

While I was cleaning, I question, can I read all of them before I die? It is possible. But since I am always adding to my collection, it seems impossible.

As I give it some more study, the doorbell rang. *"Great. I'm in the middle of the shelf."*

I was going to ignore it when the doorbell rang again. "Alright, I'm coming for Christ's sake," I yell, putting the book I had just finished back on the shelf and then go to answer the door.

When I opened the door, a tall gentleman, somewhat hunched over, shrouded in a black cloak with the hood up so you can't see his face, stands before me.

"A little warm for this type of clothing, don't you think?" I ask him.

"I'm quite comfortable, thank you," he responds.

"Glad to hear it. You realize Halloween is still a couple of months off?"

"Yes, this is true," he answers. "This has nothing to do with Halloween."

"Well, that's a relief. What can I do for you? I'm sorry, but I didn't get your name."

"That's because I didn't give it, Jackson."

"How do you know my name, but I know not yours?" I ask him.

"Don't be silly, Jackson. You are aware of who I am," he says as he extends his hand.

I accept it to shake it. It is stone cold, weathered. As I shake it, he tells me, "I… am Death."

I've heard the phrase *'when Death comes knocking'* but never took it literally.

"Right," I tell the cloaked figure as I attempt to release my grip.

I find it impossible as my hand turns purple and an icy feeling creeps up my arm.

Death speaks, "Like so many, Jackson, you do not understand until your eyes see. Your body feels. Do you understand now?"

"I see your point, sir. If it is my time, will you do me the courtesy and allow me to finish my chore? Allow me to die in my office where I go to find comfort?"

"This, I can do," answers Death.

"Then please, come in," says Jackson.

Death releases his grip and enters Jackson's home. Jackson closes the door and returns to his office to finish his task.

Death follows.

2

Death enters the office and lowers his hood.

Jackson observes Death has white hair strung out like Doc Brown's from *Back To The Future*. His face is scrunchy, a cross between *The Tall Man* from *Phantasm* and *The Crypt Keeper*. Never a delightful combination.

Jackson goes on finishing the shelf he is on as Death peruses the titles of the books on the shelves.

"An impressive collection," says Death. "Quite an ensemble. Almost every Stephen King, a favorite of mine as well. Tolkien and C. S. Lewis, very classy. Rowling, Gabaldon, Hubbard, Martin, with a mix of politics from Limbaugh, Hannity, and O'Reilly. Very nice choices. I see you also picked up a couple from Richard Chizmar. Loved *Chasing The Boogeyman*. I hoped he was writing about me. Wait, that's a spoiler. And what collection isn't complete without Poe! I loved when I got a hold of him! *Exquisite!*"

"Thank you... I guess," says Jackson. "I was pondering whether I could read them all before I die when you rang. Guess you answered that question by showing up at my door."

Death raises an eyebrow with interest.

"That sounds like an interesting proposition, Jackson."

He is silent for what seems like hours, then asks, "How many books do you read in a year?"

Jackson ponders Death's question. "I would say about six per year. With the time I have, I average a book every couple of months."

"And you have two hundred twenty-three on these shelves."

"That is correct. With another six coming in the next few months."

"So, would it be accurate to state you would have around two hundred forty by year's end?"

"That would be an accurate assessment. Since I am always purchasing new ones."

"As any good book connoisseur would," comments Death.

"I figure it would take me another forty-two years to read them all, including those I have on order."

Death scratches his chin and asks, "And how many of what you own have you read?"

"Forty-three of them," answers Jackson.

Death laughs. "You are so typical, Jackson. Keep buying more books with the intention you will read them one day, and one day never comes. I like this challenge."

"Challenge?" asks Jackson.

"Yes. I have a little proposition for you. Do you accept it?"

With no understanding of what he's getting himself into, Jackson answers, "If I get to live, then yes, I accept. What is this proposition?"

"I will grant you your desire. You will live until you read everything you have on these shelves. I will also permit those that are coming. In addition, I will give you one year to add to your collection. When the year's up, your collection is complete. No more purchases or additions. Also, from this moment on, you must read six books a year *and* under no circumstances may you read any book you have already read. These are my terms. Do you accept them?"

Jackson considers the terms Death has given to him. He questions, "What about books that are released after that year?"

"So long as you ordered them during that year's grace period, I will accept them, but no others. So, Suntup Editions would fall under this category."

"Then I accept your gracious proposition," says Jackson as he shakes Death's hand, sealing the deal.

"This is going to be interesting," says Death as he pulls an hourglass from his cloak. "Your year starts now, Jackson. When the sand runs out, so does your book buy."

Death pulls his hood back over his head. "Enjoy your reading, Jackson," he says as he leaves.

Until next we meet, Jackson echoes hauntingly throughout the room as Death disappears.

3

Jackson wastes little time over the next year adding to his collection. He purchases the latest works from the authors he's been collecting; every Suntup Edition that's announced; classic literature he's always wanted; and others that pique his interest when he spots them, averaging three new books a week.

He also honors his reading agreement.

When the sands of the hourglass run dry a year later, he has read his required six books, putting his total read to forty-six of the now three hundred ninety-eight titles in his collection.

Take away the forty-six he has read, and the six a year he needs to continue to read to live up to Death's proposition, Jackson figures it'll be at least another sixty to seventy years before he sees Death's ugly mug again.

That's a deal. He'll be well over a hundred when that happens. Reading to stay alive. It's a great thing.

So, Jackson thought.

4

What Death counts on is a concept called temptation. Jackson didn't factor this in his decision making. I mean, let's face facts. If he could reread the books he read before making the deal with Death, it adds five, six, or more years to his life.

Now, that is a great idea. But how to do it? Jackson comes up with the answer without thinking of the consequences. After finishing *NOS4A2* by Joe Hill, Jackson picks up Stephen King's *The Green Mile: The Complete Serial Novel.*

Jackson sits down to read the book. As he does, the room grows dark and cold. The book in his hand disintegrates, turning to dust. It blows away in the icy breeze as Death appears before him.

"I thought we agreed, Jackson, that we would not reread previous books already read," states Death.

"If you wish to get technical, I am not rereading a previous book," Jackson tells Death.

"Please enlighten me," says Death. "You have read *The Green Mile,* have you not?"

"Yes, and no. I have read *The Green Mile* as the serial novels as they came out. Six individual books of which I have read. This is the complete serial novel. Though the same story as an individual book I have not read."

Death stands silent. He can't believe that Jackson outwitted him on this. But one doesn't cheat Death without consequences.

"Clever," he tells Jackson. "Are you still on pace with your reading goal for this coming year?"

"Yes, I am, as per our arrangement," answers Jackson.

Death looks over the collection that Jackson assembled over his year. He tells Jackson, "I'll permit this indiscretion this time. I warn you, don't do it again. You said you were on *pace* for your six this year?"

"Yes," says Jackson.

"Magnificent," says Death. He turns to leave, telling Jackson, "Perhaps you should pick it up a bit. For being too clever!"

"I'll do my best."

"Oh, yes, Jackson. I know you will," Death says to him and disappears from the room.

5

Jackson didn't pick up on Death's cryptic message. It didn't become apparent to him until a month later.

He notices he'd been reading more than usual. In the last two weeks alone, Jackson had read four books. Two were around two hundred pages. However, the other two Jackson selected were thousand-page monsters.

Death has also made sure that Jackson wouldn't attempt a reread. Once Jackson finished a book, he notices its ghost-like. It looks like it's on the shelf, but when he goes to touch it, his hand passes through it.

Jackson's reading continues at a sped-up pace.

A scary one at that.

Four books every two weeks became eight. Eight became sixteen in the following month. It reaches the point where the following month Jackson is reading a book per day and at a speed reader's pace.

With all that reading, Jackson thought he may forget what he read. That isn't the case. He remembers everything he read, still works, and sleeps, to his surprise. How, he isn't sure.

All Jackson knew was he couldn't make himself slow down or stop.

6

A year later, Jackson closes the cover of the last book to read. He goes to place it on the shelf and finds Death in his path.

"Why, Jackson, so nice to see you. What did you choose for your last book?" asks Death.

"*Later* by Stephen King," replies Jackson.

"What a fitting title to leave on," says Death as he tells Jackson, "It is time. Shall we go?"

Jackson complains, "It's only been three years since we made the deal! I added to the collection! This conversation should not occur for at least sixty years."

"Yes, that is true," says Death as he explains, "Except you tried to cheat me. I don't take kindly to those sorts of things. However, Jackson, even though you thought you were being *clever*, I accepted your explanation, and I upheld my end of the bargain."

"How!" snaps Jackson.

"Jackson, I informed you I would not come to claim you till you had read every book in your collection. I even allowed you to add to it. Gave you a sporting chance. You did just that. You read every single book. I just increased your habit a bit."

"A bit! It was more than that, Death!"

Death smiles. He tells Jackson, "A good book hooks you right from the start. It draws you in. The world around you vanishes so you won't stop reading it. Doesn't matter the length of the book, you read it in no time. Jackson, in three years you have read three hundred and ninety-eight books. We should call Guinness, but I digress. In what you've read, you learned; lived multiple lives; and visited places you could only dream of. I would call that a wonderful and full life."

Before Jackson can say anything else, Death touches him on the forehead, and he falls to the floor. As he loses consciousness and dies, Jackson realizes Death's words ring true.

He has lived a full life, even without his books.

Death also granted his dying wish; he allowed Jackson to die among them.

1ST
FLOOR

A Note To The Would-Be Author

Becoming an author is not a simple process.

If you think lightning is going to strike and you're instantly going to become the next Stephen King, J. K. Rowling, George R. R. Martin, or whoever your favorite author is… think again.

When I asked if he had any advice for an aspiring author like me, author Richard Chizmar's response was… *"It's a long and bumpy road. Embrace the process."*

There were no truer words ever spoken.

At a recent book signing for my first self-published titles, and prior to this novel being published by an actual publisher, a young lady asked me what advice I'd give to her as an aspiring author.

I felt honored that someone was asking for my advice. Until now I've been self-published, but everyone must start somewhere.

My response? Whatever you do, *never*, and I mean *never*, give up no matter what. It isn't something that will happen overnight. It takes time and a lot of patience. Stay positive and focus on the good.

If you sell one book at a signing, hand out one business card. If you talk to one person about who you are as an author and your passion for writing, then it was a success.

Remember, every book you sell, business card you hand out, or person you speak with is another person you got your work out to and into their hands. If the individual enjoys your work, they'll tell others. Word of mouth is a powerful tool. It seems like such a small step. Though simple, it can lead to something much bigger.

Write the story you want, not the one others want you to write. Never compromise. Your audience will know how impassioned you are for the story as they read it.

And if you ever get writer's block… listen to Christmas music! It works.

Trust me.

Carlton Wolverton

Carlton Wolverton
Author

EPILOGUE

The Book Signing

Charlin's Book Nook – 1 Year Later

"That is how this novel came to fruition, ladies and gentlemen," states Carlton. "I would like to thank you all for coming out this evening. I'm pleased to answer questions and will sign your books afterward."

Carlton looks over at Melisa, the store's event coordinator.

He informs the audience, "I believe Melisa has a few instructions for you on how things will proceed, so I will turn it over… Melisa."

"Thank you, Mr. Wolverton, for the wonderful insight into your debut novel," says Melisa. She explains as Carlton gets a drink of water, "As Mr. Wolverton stated, he will take a few questions before the signing event starts. To keep things moving, we ask that you have your vouchers ready for Linda and Dave as you line up. You are welcome to take photos and chat with Mr. Wolverton as he signs your book, though we ask that you keep it short, so that everyone has an ample opportunity with him."

Melisa pauses for a moment, seeing if Carlton is ready. He gives her a nod, then she tells the audience, "I turn it back to over our author, Mr. Carlton Wolverton."

The audience gives him a round of applause.

"Thank you, Melisa," says Carlton. "First question, anyone?"

A young man, in the center of the audience, raises his hand immediately. Carlton notices and calls upon him. "You, young man."

"It's obvious you survived the fall, since you are standing here before us," states the young man. "I'm sure everyone here is curious about *how* you survived it?"

"I have to say that it was luck and divine intervention," answers Carlton. He expands, "I've read that people can survive such a catastrophe by doing many things. In my case, the elevator's emergency braking system engaged as I reached the first floor. The jarring stop took me off my feet and I hit the floor. Aside from a few bumps and bruises, I walked away unscathed."

As Carlton takes another sip of water, he points to a young lady near the front audience.

She asks, "This is your debut novel with Chapbook Press. Weren't you initially going to release your last self-published title first? And if I might also inquire, what of your other self-published titles? Will Chapbook Press be publishing them?"

"Don't you just love how much information you can get these days?" asks Carlton. "Yes, my last self-published title was to have been my debut. In the incident's wake when Mr. Lewis checked on me to ensure that my future relationship with Chapbook Publications wouldn't be affected. Yeah right! This was my chance of a lifetime. I described my idea born from that experience, and he felt we ought to proceed with it as an introduction."

"As to your second question, Chapbook is currently reviewing my previous self-published titles to determine which ones will be best for full publication."

"Does that mean some of them may never achieve full publication? That would be a shame," adds the young lady.

"That may be the case," says Carlton. "But that isn't a bad thing. Treat titles without full publication as unique, especially if autographed. If you own one, you might boast about meeting the author and owning one of his novels from before he became famous. The possibility exists they may become a collector's item one day."

Melisa interrupts before Carlton can take the next question.

"Because of time, only one more question," she says.

"You, sir," calls Carlton to a gentleman in the back of the audience.

"Thank you, Mr. Wolverton, for coming out this evening to do this," says the gentleman. "I've read just over half of your book and am really enjoying the variety of stories that you have written."

"Thank you, sir, it's much appreciated," responds Carlton.

"What happened to the thirtieth story? You titled your book *30 Storeys*, yet there are only twenty-nine."

"Ah, this is *the* question that I was expecting this evening," says Carlton. "The answer is rather simplistic. I fell twenty-nine floors. However, the prologue and the epilogue explain the narrative around those twenty-nine stories. Thus, they serve as the thirtieth story."

"That's brilliant," admits the gentleman. "I didn't think of it in that manner. Nice twist."

The gentleman sits as Carlton closes by saying, "Again, thank you all for coming out this evening. I've realized a cherished dream. Thank you for your support and I look forward to doing this again. Have a good evening, everyone!"

The audience applauds as Carlton leaves the podium.

Melisa directs him toward the prepared signing table. It's stacked with multiple copies of his book and plenty of pens.

As Carlton sits down and gets comfortable, he looks out to see at least a hundred people, perhaps more, lining up to meet him and get their books signed. What a difference from his self-publishing signings, though he cherishes all of them. Those people came out of curiosity. He had to sell them on the books. That formed the foundation of his success. A fact that Carlton swears he will never forget.

Carlton picks up his pen, looking up at his first reader. "Thank you for coming this evening," he tells her as he signs his first book as a *published* author.

STOREY
NOTES

"Storey" Notes

For those who have read any of my previous novels, I'm sure you are wondering what happened to the Author's Note that follows the conclusion of the book. Don't fret, it's on deck right after this section.

I changed things up a bit for this book and steal a page (no pun intended) from a couple of other authors whose books I've recently read. Both Richard Chizmar's *The Long Way Home* and Brian James Freeman's *Walking With Ghosts* (both I recommend, by the way) have a section at the end of the book called Story Notes.

In Story Notes, the author shares their insights and explains with the reader how a story came to fruition with the reader. It's a behind-the-scenes look at the writing process. I always enjoy learning how stories come to pass. I thought it might be fun to give it a whirl myself, letting you, the reader, know how my stories came about.

So, with no further ado…

Move… Or Get Run Over—This story stems from an actual incident that happened between my sister and me when we were younger. I was a bit of a daredevil while riding my bike, especially when leaving the house. Thought of my bike as a Colonial Viper from *Battlestar Galactica* (one of my favorite shows); the driveway, my launch tube. Naturally, speed was crucial. I'd *blast* out of the driveway and onto the street, either to hit the party store or meet friends. Take that mentality and combine it with a sister who decided it would be fun to play *"Chicken"* as her brother tore down the driveway one day. The results of *"Chicken"* are exactly as the title of the story suggests.

Michigan Theory—People who live in Michigan have a saying… *"If you don't like the weather, wait five minutes, it will change."* There's truth to this. Michigan weather is so unique and unpredictable, you can literally have all four seasons in a single day. In a few hours, sunny can turn to snowy. Not only is the weather unique, but how we Michiganders handle it is also distinctive. *Michigan Theory* is my interpretation of this based on my lifetime of observation living here.

The Turkey Tradition—As an assignment in my 11th grade English class in 1988, we were to write an original story about our traditions at Thanksgiving. I remember it got quite a laugh and an A+ grade for its originality. Found it during file cleaning and recognized it had to be in the book. It's kind of corny, but it's one of my first stories I wrote, long before I ever dreamed of becoming a writer.

Shooter's Trivia Tuesday—My good friend Brit gave me the inspiration for this one. Ran into her one day while she was visiting her parents and I asked her how she was enjoying life in Chicago. She imparted she loved her place, school was going well, and she enjoyed her job. Brit's only complaint… the bar where she worked had seen its share of violence lately. Seems they had difficulties during their trivia nights, and some patrons had gotten shot. My mind quickly conceived a premise: what if it was part of the trivia game? Who was going to get shot? That's how you won.

Gordie Dyer—Back in 2016, I met a fellow author through a mutual group. We were both members on *Facebook*, if I am not mistaken. A friendship developed between us over a few weeks as we communicated back and forth, bouncing ideas and tips off one another to assisting us both in our journey as authors. One day while chatting, she invited me to be part of a group where we (four authors) would collaborate in writing a novel based on a story idea she had about a world without art. The working title was *Art Apocalypse*. The concept of this collaboration was that each author would write an initial chapter introducing his or her character. Next, the authors would write a subsequent chapter, further developing his or her character and setting them on a collision course with one of the other author's characters. Characters unite as the authors collaborate on chapters, embarking on a joint journey. Finally, when all four authors' characters are together, each author would contribute another chapter, bringing us closer to the story's finish. We spent weeks in group chats, constructing the world and discussing how things would flow, and then we set parameters for writing deadlines. The first chapters progressed smoothly. However, during the second round of chapters, the train flew off the rails. Too many chiefs who couldn't agree. In the end, we abandoned the project, leaving an interesting story unresolved. I wrote two chapters for this book. *Gordie Dyer* was one of them. The way I concluded the chapter makes it a fitting addition to this collection. Someday, it may reunite with its fellow chapter in my story.

You're A Poor Excuse For A Pavlovian Dog—Here is another story whose origins come from a previous job I had. It's not a bad thing to have a passionate owner who ensures top-notch customer service. The person's eccentricity added a whole extra dimension to something as basic as greeting customers in the store, despite their business savvy.

The Jekyll & Hyde Secretary—My mother was unique. I worked with her early in my career. You got upset at home, also at work. Except at work, it was necessary to temper it, especially when assisting a customer. She effortlessly switched from reprimanding an employee for a mistake to being courteous while talking to a customer, only to return to finish addressing the employee. It was rather amusing to witness, except, of course, when you were on the receiving end.

Germ O Phobia—During the pandemic of Wu Han Flu (what I call Covid as it sounds less intimidating and is fun to say), we all took extra precautions in public… wearing masks and carrying hand sanitizer. Some, however, took it to the extreme. I encountered one of those people while on vacation in Salem, Massachusetts, in October 2021.

G.W.M. - Certain individuals always leave an impression on you in your professional life. Mine was the first time I met a new regional manager. Though stern, he wanted the best for every employee. He had no hesitation in passing his knowledge and experience on to those who wanted to succeed and be their best. Using strengths and weaknesses, he tactfully molded people to bring out their best. You may have taken his methods the wrong way, but if you sat back and thought about it, you realized just what he was doing. Then you went and thanked him for it. He helped mold me. So, Greg, this one's for you!

60 Miles Per Hour Through McDonald's Parking Lot—An incident that will live in infamy! After my parents divorced, my mother decided Northern Michigan wasn't big enough for her and my father. So, she took an opportunity with the company she was with and moved us to Grand Rapids, Michigan. We drove as far as my grandparents' house in Reed City and stayed the night. The following day, we headed to Grand Rapids to meet the movers at our new home. On the trip down, we stopped for breakfast at the McDonald's in Big Rapids. My mother must have been famished because, as the title suggests, she whipped through the parking lot like a bat out of hell as soon as she hit it.

Turning The Tide—If you are like me, you despise those calls about your car's warranty (which you no longer own) or other solicitation calls about anything and everything. A recent reminder took me back to a time at a friend's house. She got a phone call from an insurance company trying to sell her life insurance. Initially, she played along. Then, for amusement, she toyed with the gentleman on the line. Her words to him were hilarious. The poor guy became completely speechless and hung up. I guarantee he thought twice before making his next call.

Hello, Fat Boy—A trip to *Toys R Us* for a gift. Sounds simple enough. Buying the gift was unexpectedly challenging. When my friend Chris and I got a gift for his stepbrother, this was the situation. Chris discovered an adorable toy that appeared to possess a unique consciousness, regardless of his selection. Kind of creepy situation ending with us leaving because the toy got the better of him.

The Day The Golden Mic Went Silent—On February 17, 2021, the world lost the greatest radio talk show host of all time, Rush Limbaugh. Hearing the news of his passing hit me hard. My feelings on his loss were like hearing of the passing of a close family member. I know it makes no sense. I never met him, nor did I know him personally. Yet, he was a part of my everyday life, whether it was on the radio, through his daily emails, or even through his books. It is still a significant loss. This story is my recollection of that announcement on the 1st anniversary of his passing.

The Afterthought—Do you ever feel like an outsider in your own family? You're consistently the last to know about weddings, parties, and family gatherings. Family members who should have your back would rather put a knife in it. Lose a key member of the family and you watch as other family members' true nature comes out, and it seems to be always against you. It's a rather interesting situation, and I have seen it many times. Morally, one can only tolerate so much before reaching a breaking point. I used this as the premise. A man discussed this exact experience with his psychiatrist. Turns out, the discussion took a different turn than even I expected while writing it.

We Would Be Honored If You Would Join Us—Earlier in the book you read a story entitled *Gordie Dyer*. As I explained in that Story Note for that chapter, I had written two chapters for the abandoned project of the *Art Apocalypse*. I stated at the end of that note that someday I hoped it would reunite with its fellow chapter in its own story. Well, it just so happens I decided not to wait, and it's joining this collection. I figured it would fit, since the mind of an author is always developing a story. So, why wouldn't my author character Carlton Wolverton not come up with a second chapter for a novel he felt would come to fruition as he fell to his doom? Like the chapter of *Gordie Dyer*, *We Would Be Honored If You Could*

Join Us, I feel stands well on its own. The chapter's title comes from a line out of *The Empire Strikes Back* and the premise of the chapter fits that line to a tee. Don't worry, both chapters I wrote for that abandoned project will see themselves together back-to-back as they should be in a story of their own one day.

The Corner Of Indecision—The idea for this story came about while I was traveling up to Cedar Springs, Michigan to pick up my grandson for a weekend visit. As I reached Rockford, Michigan, there's a four corner stop on M44. If you go straight on, you will arrive in Cedar Springs. Make a left at this stop and you head into Rockford. Turn right and a few miles down the road, you wind up in Greenville, Michigan. Of course, turning around and heading back the way you came takes you back to Grand Rapids, Michigan. I commented to my wife about all the decisions you could make or the indecision if you didn't know where you wanted to go. Right then in there I came up with the first line of a story… *I came upon a corner. A corner of indecision.* The story itself developed differently than what I had originally planned.

Yard Sale—Comedian Bill Engvall is famous for his line, *"Here's your sign!"* in his comedy routines. Well, a sign was the exact inspiration for Yard Sale. I was driving home one day and saw a yard sale sign on a corner. Not uncommon, except it was pointing directly into a cemetery. Over the next few days, it consistently pointed into the cemetery as I passed by. Got me wondering, perhaps the dead have sales in the dark of night without our knowledge.

Arrogance Meets Its Match—Ever work for a manager who thought they were superior to everyone? One who constantly reminded everyone of their superiority. Occasionally, someone had the knack for putting that manager in their place. A clever individual who could outsmart you in an instant, leaving you no chance to recover. This story came from one such incident at a job I once worked. Of course, I changed the names to protect the *"innocent"*.

Anatomy Challenge—To quote Thanos from *Avengers: Infinity War*, *"You're not the only one cursed with knowledge."* With a couple of subjects in high school, it wasn't a curse. My knowledge was down pat. One subject (*Anatomy and Physiology*) I excelled at. I deemed the midterm exam was a waste of my time. My teacher, Mr. Bultmann, thought otherwise. Therefore, a challenge arose. Succeed, no final exam at the end of the semester. Fail and crow would be on the menu, among other things, for my arrogance.

A "Lion King" Tale—My niece made the announcement at the end of May that she and her husband were expecting in mid-October. Weeks later, my wife and I received an invitation to her baby shower and the opportunity to pass along my original Disney soundtrack to the film *The Lion King* presented itself. That soundtrack is something special that she and I shared. About an hour before the baby shower, I sat down, put that soundtrack on, and wrote the short tale/note (call it what you will) to her to accompany the soundtrack and a Dr. Suess book for her baby's library.

The Imagination Of A 5-Year-Old—My grandson was the inspiration for this story. He saw me trimming up my beard and mustache, and decided that I needed a *haircut* as well. He informed me he was a barber. I came to him for a haircut. Each comment built upon the previous one until he had woven a cute little narrative, which sounded something like an old Abbott and Costello routine.

The "Wahenee" Splash—Watch wrestling at some point, and you will see a move called a splash. The wrestler usually positions his opponent particularly, climbs to the top rope, then jumps off, flattening himself/herself out on the way down and *splashing* the opponent. Several wrestlers have performed this move. But have you ever seen a twenty-pound cat do it purposefully onto an unsuspecting five-pound dog? It was a spectacle to witness. Telling the story play-by-play makes it more interesting and comical.

A Visit From Krampus—A 6-Year-Old's Revenge—In Alpine tradition, Saint Nicholas comes on the eve of his feast day, December 5, giving gifts to good boys and girls. Krampus, who punishes the naughty boys and girls, accompanies him, beating them with birch rods. Children will misbehave regardless of the season. It's just their nature, as they still need to mature. Should we cancel Christmas and its magical joy for such a reason? Hell no! You don't do that. Considering I nearly witnessed this with a family member, it made me wonder... what if the kid had had enough? Mom and dad are naughty in the kids' eyes. Have the kid who believes in the stories of Saint Nicholas and Krampus his grandfather has passed on to him and have faith in them to the point they come to fruition. Then punish the parents for their behavior and not the other way around. That sounded interesting. It comes down to the adage that turnabout is fair play.

The Demons Always Catch Up—Each of us has our own personal demons... regrets from past actions. The stone-cold truth is that we cannot alter the past. To learn from the past helps us avoid repeating mistakes and keeps the demons at bay. Some, (this story applies to one I knew), however, never learn. They persist on an inescapable path, where the pursuing demons eventually engulf them.

A Tale Of St. Nicholas—In 2007, while I was doing some initial research on my third novel, *Saint Nick*, I came across a movie that was in production call *Nicholas Of Myra*. This film recounts Saint Nicholas's life, the inspiration for our modern Santa Claus. I've been a big supporter of this film and have become good friends with Gerald Hartke, the writer and director. In 2018, Gerald ran a campaign to help raise funds for the film. Those that donated a specific amount received a poster for the film along with other film related items. The script's first ten pages, Nicolas Of Myra, were among those items. In conversations with Gerald, I petitioned him as a potential candidate to novelize his script. I believe it is a great opportunity for me as a self-published author to potentially get published.

That would then open other possibilities. He was very open to the idea and gave it his consideration. Naturally, he sought work samples; his investors needed to choose the ideal author; a process I understood involved multiple candidates. Initially, I offered a copy of my third novel I published, *Saint Nick*, being the best example for his review because of the subject. Then it hit me. The best way to show him and his investors I was the author for the job… adapt the part of the script I had. I adapted the first pages into the book's first chapter. I then submitted it to Gerald for his consideration. Since I've submitted it, I have heard nothing. But expected because of recent Focus Group updates revealing understandable setbacks. Much like the chapters of *Gordie Dyer* and *We Would Be Honored If You Would Join Us* (See Relative Story Notes Above), I didn't want this effort to sit idle and never see the light of day. Gerald approved; thus, this novel unveils it. Like *Gordie Dyer* and *We Would Be Honored If You Would Join Us*, perhaps one day this chapter will see its rightful place in the novelization of *Nicholas Of Myra*. Enjoy it in the meanwhile.

May The 4th Be With You—May 1977 I was just shy of six. On a school night no less, my father took me downtown to our little one screen movie theatre, complete with a balcony, for a movie night. The film we went to see, a science fiction film called *Star Wars*. We did not know this movie would become such a worldwide phenomenon and inspiration. The memory lingers, vivid and unforgettable.

The Master's Hand—When you visit *Bronner's CHRISTmas Wonderland* in Frankenmuth, Michigan and make a purchase, they put a small *Good News Tracts* booklet in your bag. These little booklets contain stories that tie into a Biblical meaning. One of these booklets inspired this story called *"The Touch Of The Master's Hand"*. It's a story of a violin up at auction. Initially worthless, until a man appears, cleans, tunes, and transforms it into a wonder. The explanation is that the Master's hand gave it the touch. God's hand is clear in this story, channeled through a musician. I find some of my stories come with such ease and practically write themselves.

I am simply a vessel for the story to flow. *Saint Nick* is the most notable example of this. Is it because of the passion I have for Saint Nicholas? Or did I also experience the touch of the Master's hand?

'Till Book Do Us Part—The idea for this story came to me while I was cleaning the bookshelves in my office one Sunday afternoon. Right now, I have 164 books, and I've read roughly a quarter of them. Problem is… I am always adding new ones. I wondered if I'd ever read them all before I *die*d. Then I thought, what if I could live until I read them all? Wouldn't that be something?

A Note To The Would Be Author—On August 3, 2019, I had a book signing at Bookbrokers & Kramer's Café in Traverse City, Michigan. "Doc", the owner, has a deep passion for books and the art of writing. He supports all authors, especially those who, like me, are self-published. Doc asks every author who has a signing at Bookbrokers to write an entry in his journal. The journal allows authors to gain insight and encouragement from their peers. This story is the entry I wrote that day. I thought it would be the best way to round out the *30 Storeys*.

AUTHOR'S
NOTE

Author's Note

A story's beginnings can come from anywhere, as the story notes show. *30 Storeys* is no different.

Would you believe the inspiration for *30 Storeys* came from a commercial promoting a television show called *The Misery Index*?

I saw a commercial for the show. The host shared a tale of a man who was in an elevator that took a 30-story plunge with a group of comedians. When asked if he survived, the response was yes. One comedian then joked; "Guess he'll have 30 stories to tell."

After hearing that, I thought it would be an interesting idea for a book. That was in 2023. Fast forward two years to 2025 and you now hold in your hand my 8th book, *30 Storeys*.

For this book, I tried something different. My earlier novels each presented a single, developing narrative. This novel, however, turned out to be many stories within a story. Sounds weird but makes sense now that you have read it (or will instead of reading the Author's Note first).

Short stories I found are a bit more difficult to write since you need to convey the story in short order. Many of the stories within are based on fond memories of my past along with many that are one-of-a-kind. The result: a book that features several stories—both nostalgic and new. Unfortunately, there were a few that didn't make the final cut. Don't worry though. I can always publish them in a future short story collection or develop them into full novels, who's to say.

They say *Practice makes perfect*. With each book, my writing and editing skills improve. Perhaps one day, I will be as good as The Master (Stephen King) himself. Till then I am still perfecting my craft. This book's existence, however, owes a debt to:

Back in late 2018, early 2019, I went to Charlin's Book Nook which is a local small business in the Frankenmuth River Place Shops. I spoke with the owner, Linda Strappazon, about setting up a book signing with them. The rest, as they say, is history. Since that time, Linda, Melisa and Dave of Charlin's have become one of my biggest supporters. Thank you all for your support and encouragement. My readership's growth stems from my Signing Saturdays at Charlin's and their ongoing promotion of my work. I appreciate everything you do for me more than you know! You all make me feel like part of the family.

Though I may have adapted it into story form, I can't take the credit for the chapter of *A Tale Of St. Nicholas*. Gerald Hartke, script writer of *Nicholas of Myra – The Untold Origin Of An Age-Old Legend* deserves that credit. If you read the Story Notes prior to the Author's Note, you know the back story for this chapter. If you didn't, I recommend it. Either way, my thanks to my good friend, fellow writer, follower of St. Nicholas, and fellow Brother In Red, Gerald Hartke, for allowing me to use my adaption of his work in this novel. Regardless of whether I get to novelize the full script (fingers still crossed), for me it was a great exercise and a way for me to continue to polish my skills and hone my craft. Your film will become a timeless classic. Thank you, my friend. It's appreciated more than you will ever know.

No book of mine is complete until it has been through the editing process with my editor Hazel Benedict, otherwise known as *Helen with the Blood Red Pen*! No matter how sophisticated an editing program I use, it pales compared to her skills. She excels; her editing skills surpass even those of today's leading authors. I couldn't manage without her and you are like a second mother to me. Thank you for all that you do.

I have a group of friends that I've been through thick and thin with. We support one another unconditionally. I refer to them as *The Goonies*... Tammy Foster, Jeff and Elizabeth Van't Hof, Aaron Sanford, and Richard Charles Goebel.

For this novel, someone who is also a big supporter of mine needs to be acknowledged, Mr. James Ross. Thank you, my friend, not only for your friendship but for your support of me as a writer as well. Means the world to me.

Being blessed with one *Guardian Angel* is a gift. I'm uncertain what to call four. Whatever the term, God must have truly blessed me, or I must've done something extraordinary to deserve that. My four of them watching over me: Carolynn Califf (Mother), Royce Saunders (Grandfather), Eithel Saunders (Grandmother), and Gary Saunders (Godfather & Uncle). I think of them often, miss them daily, and keep them always near to my heart. Hope I am doing them proud.

Last, but not least, my wife, Angela Kroupa. You are my biggest supporter through thick and thin and you put up with a lot from me. I can't put into words how much you loving me, being my rock, and keeping me grounded means to me. As I tell you so often, *truly,* you are the best.

As always, the final thank you goes out to you, my readers. Thank you for your continued support. I appreciate it more than you will ever know. You make it possible for me to do the job I love to do, *write.* It's not work when you're passionate; true?

Till next time…

Brandon G. Kroupa
Grand Rapids, Michigan
June 2025

ABOUT
THE
AUTHOR

ABOUT THE AUTHOR

After hearing the song, "The Legend" by Steve Cook while traveling to visit his dad's home in Traverse City, Michigan in 2005, Brandon G. Kroupa found inspiration for his first novel, *The Seventh Year*, which he published seven years later (no pun intended) on April 7, 2012.

Since that novel's publication 13 years ago, Mr. Kroupa hasn't slowed down.

He has since gone on to self-publish six other novels through The Chapbook Press, within Schuler Books (A Local Independent Bookstore in Grand Rapids, Michigan), including his most recent novel, "What Happened To The 'Muth'?", a historical fiction story about Frankenmuth, Michigan.

You'll find him every "Writing Wednesday" (his lingo), at his "home" office writing his next novel.

As a self-published author, he has a unique approach and outlook which is, "If I sell one book at a signing or even hand out one business card, then that signing was a success." You may ask "But it was only one?" True, but that one might tell others who will get them interested and then that turns to two and so on. It works, trust him.

His books are stories inspired by songs, life-events, and personal interests.

When he is not writing, Mr. Kroupa enjoys trips to his favorite city… Frankenmuth, Michigan, catching a hockey game, reading the latest

Stephen King novel, and spending time with his wife and three grandchildren.

He lives in Grand Rapids, Michigan with his wife Angela.

Please visit the author's website at: www.bkrowriter.com and follow him on Facebook @bkrowwriter.